# THE
# NOVICE

ALSO BY THICH NHAT HANH

*No Death, No Fear*
*Living Buddha, Living Christ*
*Fragrant Palm Leaves*
*Being Peace*
*For a Future to Be Possible*
*The Heart of the Buddha's Teaching*
*The Heart of Understanding*
*The Long Road Turns to Joy*
*Love in Action*
*The Miracle of Mindfulness*
*Old Path, White Clouds*
*Peace Is Every Step*
*Anger*
*True Love*
*Art of Power*
*Savor*
*Peace Is Every Breath*

# THE NOVICE

*A Story of True Love*

THICH NHAT HANH

HarperOne
*An Imprint of HarperCollinsPublishers*

HarperOne

HarperCollins books may be purchased for educational, business, or sales promotional use. For information please write: Special Markets Department, HarperCollins Publishers, 10 East 53rd Street, New York, NY 10022.

HarperCollins Web site: http://www.harpercollins.com

HarperCollins®, 📖®, and HarperOne™ are trademarks of HarperCollins Publishers.

FIRST EDITION

Library of Congress Cataloging-in-Publication Data is available.

ISBN: 978–0–06–200583–0

11 12 13 14 15   RRD (H)   10 9 8 7 6 5 4 3 2 1

# CONTENTS

# THE
# NOVICE

*Chapter One*

# ABANDONED CHILD

Kinh Tam had just finished sounding the last bell of the evening chant when the young novice heard the wailing of a baby. Kinh Tam thought, "That's strange!" Releasing the bell, the novice quietly stepped over to the doorway of the bell tower and looked down at the hillside just in time to see Thi Mau in a light brown nam than, a long shirt commonly worn by Vietnamese women, holding a crying newborn in her arms. She gazed up in the novice's direction.

An alarming thought flashed in Kinh Tam's mind. "Thi Mau must have given birth to the child and is now coming up here to leave it in my care."

Waves of turbulent feelings arose rapidly within. Novice Kinh Tam reviewed the precarious situation. "I've taken the monastic vows of a novice. I've just been accused of having a sexual affair with Thi Mau, making her pregnant, and not owning up to the alleged offense." The thoughts tumbled on. "Who can possibly understand the predicament I'm facing? Doesn't anyone see the great injustice being done to me? Even though my teacher, the abbot of this temple, loves me, even though my two Dharma brothers care deeply for me, who knows whether they have doubts about my heart? And now the baby is here. Stubbornly refusing to bring the newborn to its true father, Thi Mau has brought it here to the temple. Everyone who already suspected that I'm the child's father will surely misconstrue my taking in the newborn. They will say I've admitted my guilt. What will my teacher think? How will my Dharma brothers react? And the people in the village?"

Novice Kinh Tam finally concluded, "Maybe I should go down to meet Thi Mau and advise her to be brave, to tell her parents the name of the real father, and to take the baby to him instead." Kinh Tam stepped down from the bell tower, all the while silently invoking the name of Buddha. The novice had a lot of confidence in the healing energy of loving-kindness embodied by the Buddha. Surely the Buddha's wisdom could be a guide through this very difficult period. The novice intended to use gentle, kind words to advise Thi Mau, to help her see a more admirable way to handle this situation. But as the novice stepped out of the bell tower, Thi Mau had already run away, quite far down the hillside. She shot through the temple gates like an arrow and disappeared into the hills thick with evergreens. At that very moment, the newborn, wrapped in many layers of white cotton cloth and abandoned on the steps leading to the bell tower, burst out in heart-wrenching cries.

Kinh Tam quickly ran over to pick up the baby. From deep within, the novice felt the budding of a new love. The nurturing instinct sprang up as a powerful source of energy. "This child is not being cared for or acknowledged by anyone. His father does not recognize him, and his own mother has just abandoned him. His paternal grandparents don't even know he is present on this Earth. If I don't take him into my care, then who will?" thought the novice. "I claim to be a monk, a person practicing to be more compassionate, so how can I have the right or the heart to desert this child?" The novice grew adamant. "Let them gossip, let them suspect, let them curse me! The newborn needs someone to take care of him and raise him. If I don't do it, then who will?"

With tears streaming down, Kinh Tam lovingly hugged and cuddled the baby. The novice's heart was filled at once with both great sadness and the sweet nectar of compassion. Kinh Tam sensed that the baby was getting hungry and thought immediately of Uncle and Aunt Han ("Rarity"), a couple living in the village below the hill on which the temple stood. Aunt Han had given birth to a baby just a fortnight ago. The most important thing to do now was to take this baby down to the village and beg that he be nursed. Uncle and Aunt Han regularly attended temple services, and they were on good terms with all the novices. Surely the good woman would be willing to share some of her milk to feed this unfortunate child.

Kinh Tam wrapped the cotton layers more snugly around the baby to keep him warm. Then the novice carried the little baby through the gate and down along the path leading to the village below, fully attentive to each step and each breath.

"Tomorrow morning, my teacher and my two Dharma brothers will undoubtedly question me for taking in the baby," the novice pondered silently. "And I will answer: Dear teacher, you have taught me that the merit to be gained through building an elaborate temple nine stories high cannot compare to that of saving the life of one person. Taking your advice to heart, I have taken in this baby to rear. I ask you, dear teacher and dear Dharma brothers, to have compassion. The baby has been neglected, abandoned, and rejected by everyone. Thi Mau left him on the steps of the bell tower last evening and then ran away without saying anything. If I had not taken him in and cared for him, the child would have died.

"'Homage to Avalokiteshvara, the bodhisattva giving aid in desperate crises.' Everyone who comes to the temple always recites verses like this with much devotion. Every one of us needs to take refuge in the Bodhisattva of Great Compassion and Loving-kindness. Yet very few of us actually practice nurturing and offering great compassion and loving-kindness in our daily lives." The novice continued reflecting. "I'm a disciple of the Buddha and the bodhisattvas; I have to practice in accord with their aspirations. I must be able to cultivate and embody the energies of great compassion and loving-kindness that are within me."

At that time, although Kinh Tam was just twenty-four years old, the novice had already twice endured great injustice. The first was being accused of attempting to kill another person. The second was being said to have transgressed the monastic vows in sleeping with Mau, the daughter of the richest family in the village, and making her pregnant. Two instances of very grave injustice. But Kinh Tam could still bear it, because the novice knew the practice of inclusiveness (magnanimity) and had learned ways to nourish loving-kindness and compassion.

In fact, the novice was not a young man at all. Kinh Tam was actually a daughter of the Ly ("Plum") family in another province. Her parents had named her Kinh ("Reverence"). Because she so strongly wished to live the monastic life, Kinh had disguised herself as a young man in order to be ordained. Buddhism had entered Giao Chau, the ancient name for what is now Vietnam, around two hundred years earlier, and the temples there were only receiving men for ordination.

Kinh had heard that long ago in India there had been numerous temples in which women could become Buddhist nuns. She often wondered, "How much longer will we have to wait before we have a temple for nuns in this country?"

She came to Dharma Cloud Temple, one of the most beautiful temples in the land, to be ordained and to live the monastic life. The temple was in the Giao Chi district, six days' travel from her home village in Cuu Chan district. Kinh hid the fact from her parents that she was practicing at Dharma Cloud Temple. She knew that if they were to learn of her ordination and whereabouts, they would intervene and beseech her to return home to them.

Just to have the teacher find out that she was a girl in disguise would be enough to have her expelled from the temple. And if she were to become unable to continue the monastic life, the suffering would be too unbearable.

From early childhood, Kinh had been very much a tomboy, always joining in the games of boys. Her parents dressed her in little boys' outfits. As she got older, they received permission for Kinh to join a classical Chinese class for young boys with the village teacher, named Bai ("Bowing"). Kinh studied very well and received better grades than many of the boys in her class.

Kinh was polite, composed, and sociable, but she was no pushover. Kinh refused to apologize if she saw that she was not at fault, even when asked to by her teacher or her parents. She would respectfully join her palms together and reason, "I cannot apologize, since I did not do anything wrong."

Some remarked that Kinh was stubborn. Maybe she was, but what could she do about the way she was? At that time, Kinh was an only child, quite cherished and, yes, a bit spoiled by her parents. This changed, though, when Kinh was seven years old and her mother gave birth to her baby brother, whom they named Chau ("Jewel").

Kinh grew more beautiful with each passing year. When she turned sixteen, many families offered their sons in marriage. Her parents had refused them all— partly because these families did not have the same so- cial status as they did, but also because they were not yet ready to let their daughter go. However, when an offer came from the parents of Thien Si ("Good Scholar"), Kinh's parents dropped all hesitation and accepted Thien Si was a son of the Dao family. At the time of the offer, he was a college student studying at the Dai Tap University and reputedly a very good student. Thien Si's parents had much prestige in the district and could trace their lineage back several centuries.

Kinh was nineteen years old and felt she was too young to get married. She had graduated from the Tieu Tap School and already was accepted at Dai Tap Uni- versity, but her parents forbade her to attend. A woman's role was to get married and raise a family, and Kinh's parents did not wish to send her off to school.

Not having much choice in the matter, Kinh had re- signed herself to continue her education by self-study at home. She read the classical Confucian *Four Books* and *Five Classics,* and also had access to religious books. The greatest fortune in her life was that she had the chance to read the sutra texts of the Buddha. She read *The Sutra of Forty-Two Chapters, The Prajnaparamita in Eight Thousand Lines, The Collection on the Six Paramitas* by Zen Master Tang Hoi, and *Dispelling Doubts* by Mouzi.

Teacher Bai was greatly interested in Buddhism, and it was he who lent those sutras and books to Kinh. Once, he even allowed her to visit his home and serve tea to three Buddhist monks whom he had invited over in order to offer them the midday meal and donations of other basic items. In her first encounter with monastics, Kinh was awestruck. The monks wore simple brown robes, and their heads were cleanly shaven. Their bearing was gentle, calm, and relaxed, while their voices conveyed much compassion. Kinh deeply wished to be able to live such a life. But she knew that she could not realize this dream, since in her country temples for nuns simply did not exist.

While reading the sutra on the six perfections, Kinh was often moved to tears. She learned of the Buddha's life and of the practices of the six perfections—generosity, mindfulness trainings, inclusiveness (magnanimity), diligence, meditation, and insight. The monastic life appealed so much to her. She saw that a monastic's heart was filled with the abundant energy of love, compassion, inclusiveness, and diligence. She regretted that she had not been born a boy and thus able to live this beautiful way of life.

And now Kinh's own parents had agreed to Thien Si's parents' proposal for marriage. Girls grew up and eventually had to get married. That was just the way things went in those days. How could she go against such a strong tradition? She hoped Thien Si would be easygoing and would not object to her yearning for knowledge or her desire to practice Buddhism.

And so, in the following spring, twenty-year-old Kinh was married into the Dao family. Thien Si was an intelligent young man who was gentle and did well in his studies. At the same time, he was a bit oversensitive, tended to indulge himself, and was not very strong or stable mentally. Many times Kinh had to gently urge him to wake up, eat, sleep, and do his studies with more regularity, but often he just could not do it, however hard he tried, even just to please her. Her in-laws slowly began to look askance at how Thien Si seemed to spend more and more of his time affectionately idle by her side. Kinh had done her best to be an ideal daughter-in-law, as her own mother had taught her to be. The last to sleep, the earliest to rise, tending to all household chores, giving utmost care to her husband's parents—there was no oversight for which Thien Si's parents could have criticized her. But they felt as if she had stolen the affection of their precious only son from them, and they bitterly resented her. For Thien Si's part, he seemed to live less like a person in his own right and more like someone else's shadow.

*Chapter Two*

# HUMILIATION

Late one night as Kinh was doing some mending, Thien Si was sitting nearby, studying. It was already quite late, but he had persisted in his reading. He then fell asleep next to his young wife. Looking over at him, Kinh saw several strands of hair in his beard growing crudely against the general direction of the rest. With the intention of trimming those few strands, she raised her sewing scissors to do so.

Unfortunately Thien Si woke up at that very moment, and with his mind still muddled from being half asleep, he saw Kinh bringing the sharp scissors toward his throat and thought she was about to kill him. Utterly terrified, Thien Si screamed for help. His parents, still awake in their bedroom next door, came running in.

They yelled, "What happened?"

Thien Si related the incident of waking to the sight of his wife putting her scissors to his throat. Both his parents exploded with rage. They accused Kinh of trying to kill her own husband. They completely refused to listen to any of her pleas for justice.

"Good grief! Why did we bring this nuisance into the family? She's a saucy daughter-in-law, a flirt, a wanton, evil woman trying to kill her husband, so that she can be with another man!" screamed the old woman.

Kinh turned toward her husband, earnestly pleading with him to clear her of his parents' false accusations. But Thien Si, overwhelmed by a state of total trauma, said nothing. He sat there crying like a man who had lost his mind altogether. Thien Si could not take control of the situation at all. He sat there like a wretched victim, totally incapable of even a tiny response.

The next morning Thien Si's parents sent a house servant to call Kinh's parents over. They seethed, "We do not dare to keep your daughter in our family any longer. Luckily, Thien Si woke up in time or else he would have lost his life. Young women these days are so deceitful. Their outer appearance seems gentle and meek, but deep inside they are hostile and malicious. Who knows, maybe she has fallen for another young man! We return her to you. Our family does not have enough 'good fortune' to keep this burden any longer!"

Kinh's parents looked over to their daughter. It was only then that she was given the chance to explain clearly what had transpired. Her voice was steady and full of respect.

Kinh's father turned to Thien Si's parents and said, "I cannot ever imagine our daughter being a murderous person. Both of you have unjustly accused her. Our daughter is a most kindhearted person."

Thien Si's mother pursed her lips, refusing to believe in Kinh's explanation, and demanded that Kinh go back home to her parents.

Kinh's mother gently prodded her daughter, "You have made a foolish mistake! You need now to bow to your parents-in-law and your husband and beg for their forgiveness."

Kinh refused. She politely answered, "I didn't do anything foolish. All I wanted to do was to trim the few stray hairs in my husband's beard. I have no heart to kill anyone. If I were at fault, I would be more than willing to bow down. But I know with all certainty that I did no wrong, so I cannot do as you advise."

And so Kinh followed her parents back home. On leaving, she only slightly bent her head toward everyone, but did not bow low. Thien Si sat silent as a statue. He had no reaction of any kind.

Kinh knew her parents were unhappy, not only because of the abrupt end of her marital life, but also
because of the scandal. Personally Kinh did not feel very
sad. She felt no anger toward Thien Si or his parents,
but was more disappointed in the way people interacted
in general. People, it seemed, were always allowing
jealousy, sadness, anger, and pride to determine their
behavior. So much suffering was caused by misunder-
standings and erroneous perceptions about one another.

In her married life over the past year, Kinh had experienced just a handful of happy moments and plenty of
difficult ones. Thien Si did not know how to really live
his life. He thought only of exams and of being a government official. He did not know how to appreciate the
gift of living with his loved ones. To him, literature and
academic studies were just a means to advance him in
society and were not in themselves sources of happiness
in life. Many times Kinh had struck up conversations
with him on literature and other subjects, but he was
only interested in the respect he could gain through his
studies and not in any inherent value they possessed. He
particularly disliked discussions on Taoism and Buddhism. To him, there was only one discipline worthy
of being called a religion, and that was Confucianism.

After returning to her parents' home, Kinh was immediately more relaxed and carefree. Besides caring for her parents, Kinh focused on studying Buddhism and overseeing the studies of her younger brother, Chau. She spent all her free time teaching herself to do sitting meditation and slow walking meditation.

She frequently visited her former teacher, Bai, to discuss Buddhism more deeply. Her teacher saw in her a true friend. Of all the people in the district, Kinh was the only one whose interest in learning and practicing Buddhism was comparable to his own. Teacher Bai told her of the large temples around the country and the scriptures being circulated. He told her of various temples where hundreds of monastics dwelled together to practice and study. Listening to him, Kinh's deep longing was rekindled. "If I were a male, I definitely would become a monk!" she thought.

*Chapter Three*

# STEPPING
# INTO
# FREEDOM

One morning, Kinh woke up very early. Unable to stifle any longer her deep desire to live a monastic life, she wrote a letter to her parents asking permission to travel for the sake of learning, and promising to return after five years of exploration. She then disguised herself as a young man, looking very bright and scholarly with a bundle of possessions slung casually over her shoulder. She left, not knowing where she would end up.

Seven days later, she arrived at Dharma Cloud Temple in Giao Chi district. The beautiful landscape surrounding the temple was peaceful and calming. The abbot was teaching an audience of about three hundred people gathered there. Everyone was listening attentively and with much respect as the abbot taught about the four factors of true love (also known as the Four Immeasurable Minds): loving-kindness, compassion, joy, and equanimity.

The young scholar arrived just as the talk began. Kinh listened zealously. Afterwards, when the teaching ended and everyone else had gone home, Kinh asked permission to consult with the reverend teacher. Prostrating deeply three times, the scholar made introductions and begged to be ordained as a monastic disciple.

The elderly abbot looked at Kinh in silence for a very long time, then calmly asked, "Where do you come from, my child? What reasons might you have for wanting to leave your home and family and become a monk?"

Palms together, the young scholar respectfully answered, "Reverend teacher, my family name is Ly, and I come from the Cuu Chan district. I began my schooling at a very young age. But I have seen that life is so impermanent. I do not find happiness or much interest in the career of a scholar or of being appointed as a minister or counselor to the king. Nor do I find happiness in married life."

The scholar continued, "Many times I have learned from my village teacher about the way of liberation, and I was given a few books on Buddhist teachings for further study. I also had the good fortune to meet with monks. Observing their free, relaxed manner and hearing their teachings about liberation moved me so much. I have dreamed for so long of becoming a monk. My journey has now brought me to this district; and after hearing your teachings, I feel a great opening of mind and heart! I bow my head deeply, appealing to your immense generosity to accept me as a monastic disciple. I vow to practice diligently, so that in the future I may be able to help everyone who suffers."

The abbot of Dharma Cloud Temple nodded. "Listening to you, it's clear you possess the good heart of a monastic. You come from a good family, and you have a solid educational foundation, the refined bearing of a scholar, and a bright future ahead of you. Another person in your position would most likely not think of giving all that up to become a monk. But since the teachings of the Buddha have opened your eyes early, I earnestly hope you will be able to fulfill the deep vow of one who has the mind of awakening, the mind of love. You may come and practice at my temple as a novice-in-training for a trial period of three months."

The abbot called for the two novices currently practicing at Dharma Cloud Temple and introduced Kinh to them. The abbot's elder disciple, Chi Tam ("Heart of Aspiration"), was twenty-six years old and had been a novice for eight years. He was of tall stature and had shining eyes under a pair of bushy eyebrows. His gait could be likened to that of a grizzly bear; it reflected enormous strength, well contained. The second novice, Thanh Tam ("Sincere Heart"), was twenty-four years old and had practiced for four years as a novice. Though his frame was slender, he was healthy and strong. He had a well-proportioned face, and his smiles were always fresh. The abbot instructed the two novices to help get the young scholar settled and oriented in the ways of life at the monastery. Kinh was very lucky to be given a small, single room in the corner of the West Hall.

In the few months of training, Kinh practiced very diligently and did tasks well. The young scholar was able to memorize and do the morning and evening chanting very fluently after studying and practicing for only a couple of weeks. Kinh bound some papers together to make a book for copying down the text of the ten vows of a novice and the novices' mindful manners. Kinh's handwriting with the brush pen was so exquisite that it drew endless praise from the elder monks, Chi Tam and Thanh Tam. Being quite knowledgeable, Kinh made comments during discussions about the teachings that also earned the new student much respect from the elder brothers and from the abbot as well. Yet Kinh always remained very humble.

All the tasks in the temple—carrying water, chopping wood, preparing vegetables, cooking, cleaning, taking care of the Buddha Hall, attending the abbot— Kinh did very thoroughly and wholeheartedly. The elder brothers cared for the new student a great deal. Brother Chi Tam, seeing that Kinh had the slight build of a scholar, shouldered more of the work needing strength. Brother Thanh Tam was also thoughtful in wanting to help Kinh in all tasks. Both had a strong desire to be near Kinh, whether to do work, to study, or to converse, because both found Kinh so fresh, gentle, intelligent, and virtuous. Kinh somehow always kept a respectful, amiable distance.

Three months later, during the annual commemoration of the Buddha's birth, Kinh was formally ordained, taking on the ten vows and the shaven head of a novice. Thus cleanly shaven and clothed in a dark brown robe of a monk, the newly ordained novice manifested the deeper beauty of a monastic, radiating so much brightness and freshness. The abbot gave the new novice the Dharma name Kinh Tam ("Reverent Heart"). This name was very meaningful and also appropriate, as Kinh Tam had much reverence for the Buddha, the spiritual patriarchs, and all other beings, including those of the animal, plant, and even mineral realms. Looking deeply, the novice saw that all life was wondrous and sacred, even the suffering of human beings. This insight just naturally made the novice always want to bow reverently before all. Ever since Kinh Tam was ordained, the Dharma Cloud Temple seemed to brighten up, and the young people of the village and other villages nearby were now visiting the temple more often and in greater numbers. Novice Kinh Tam was like a newly blooming lotus in a pond where lotuses had never been found before.

Kinh Tam had a beautiful chanting voice and had taken on the task of sounding the large bell in the tower every morning. The novice melodiously recited the poetic verses for sounding the bell, such as:

*May the sound of this bell penetrate deeply into*
 *the cosmos.*
*In even the darkest places, may living beings hear*
 *it clearly*
*so that understanding comes to their hearts,*

*and without much hardship, they transcend the*
  *cycle of birth and death.*

or:

*Listening to the bell I feel the afflictions in me*
  *begin to dissolve.*
*My mind becomes calm, my body relaxed, and a*
  *smile is born on my lips.*
*Following the sound of the bell, my breath guides*
  *me back to the safe island of mindfulness.*
*In the garden of my heart, the flower of peace*
  *blooms beautifully.*

In Dharma discussion, a period of time allotted to confer in depth about the teachings, novice Kinh Tam shared very profound insights into the written scriptures. The elder brothers, who'd had many more years of practice, listened intently and found they could learn much from what novice Kinh Tam had to share. On one occasion, the abbot himself openly praised the novice. Brother Chi Tam had to admit that, although his own Chinese character writing was beautiful, Brother Kinh Tam's character writing was indisputably livelier.

Brother Thanh Tam often asked Kinh Tam to explain further for him the difficult parts of the *Sutra of Forty-Two Chapters,* like "Practice the nonpractice, realize the nonrealizable."

Novice Kinh Tam, having already finished reading all of the *Collection on the Six Paramitas* by Master Tang Hoi, was well versed in the deeds and deep aspirations of Sakyamuni Buddha and in his past lives. The novice often retold those short stories to the elder novice monks, sharing with them the various praiseworthy deeds of the Buddha in past lives and in his life as Siddhartha Gautama. Whenever villagers, particularly the young people, came up to the temple, they had the chance to meet with the three novices and often heard novice Kinh Tam give teachings on the Dharma.

*Chapter Four*

# DELIRIUM

Thi Mau ("Wondrous") was a young maiden, the daughter of the richest family in the village. She often went with her mother up to the temple to offer incense and prostrate before the Buddha. When she first saw novice Kinh Tam, Mau was amazed. How could anyone be so elegant and genteel, with such a glowing, fresh countenance? Although Kinh Tam had a clean-shaven head and only humble monastic garments, the novice was quite refined. Even as a layperson, Kinh already had exquisite beauty and cultured bearing. Yet incredibly, after shaving the head and taking the vows, the novice became even more beautiful. From Mau's perspective, the novice's eyes sparkled more, his complexion was brighter, and purity and goodness emanated from his radiant face. An unhappy person could never demonstrate such a fresh smile, such a glowing countenance, such twinkling eyes. Everyone who looked upon Kinh Tam felt immediately refreshed and inspired. And so the young maiden Mau fell in love with the novice.

Unfortunately, Mau's love quickly became an obsessive craving. Returning home from Dharma Cloud, Mau had many sleepless nights. She was constantly haunted by the novice's image. The novice was handsome—was that why she secretly thought of him and loved him? This really could not be the reason. She had already met many handsome young men and had never reacted this way. Among the numerous young men who had extended marriage proposals via their parents, there were plenty who were quite attractive; but Mau had never experienced this kind of longing for any of them. Mau was powerless to resist this strange love. She knew that Kinh Tam was a monk and she should leave him alone, yet she simply could not suppress her longing for the novice.

Being from a rich family and endowed with beauty, Mau tended to be a bit conceited. It was very difficult for anyone to get an invitation to meet with her. If she disliked anyone, she would flatly refuse to see that person. She never imagined that anyone would not want to meet and get to know her. Yet this time, Mau's overtures were deflected. She ardently sought to see and sit with Kinh Tam, but the novice always found various reasons to avoid being with her. It was not because the novice disliked this young woman. Kinh Tam was fully engaged in observing the precepts and fine manners of a novice monk, which included not befriending and conversing with women alone in secluded places.

As time passed, Mau often stood in the novice's path either within the temple or on the dirt trails down to the village. Kinh Tam always had one excuse or another for not stopping to engage in private conversations with her. The novice had told her that she was welcome to join other young men and women who often gathered at the temple to hear and learn about the Dharma. But what Mau dreamed of was to be able to stand or to sit with the novice alone, to be able to declare her love for him and tell him she could not live without his love.

Kinh Tam soon became aware of Mau's intention. After all, Mau was not very subtle. The novice went out of his way to avoid her and the possibility of ending up in an impossible situation. The novice's deepest desire was to continue practicing as a monastic. This kind of desire is known as *bodhicitta,* the mind of bodhisattvas, of awakened beings—the mind of love. This is love that contains the spirit of kindness, compassion, joy, and equanimity; it is not a sentimental, tragic, obsessive, or sensual kind of love. To love, according to the teachings of the Buddha, is to have compassion for and to relieve the miseries of all who suffer, miseries due to sensual desires, hatred, ignorance, envy, arrogance, and doubtfulness.

Mau loved the novice. But the fact that Kinh Tam did not pursue her, did not plead for her special attention, did not show any sign of desiring her, deeply wounded her pride. Never before had any young man dealt with her in this manner. All of her suitors were so willing to chase after her and flirt with her, begging for the tiniest crumbs of loving endearments. Now she had met a person who behaved very differently indeed. Novice Kinh Tam's demeanor was so pure and noble that neither her family's prestige, nor her beauty, nor her wealth could bend him to her will. Thus she became vindictive toward Kinh Tam, even as she continued to yearn for his embrace.

It was the full-moon night of the ninth lunar month. The moon was shining ever so brightly. Mau was home alone, as her parents had not yet returned from the annual memorial service for her maternal grandparents. The late autumn night was cold and bleak. Mau could not endure the bitter loneliness engulfing her whole being. Earlier that morning, she had gone up to the

temple to offer incense, accompanied by a servant boy
named Thuong, who carried the various parcels of of-
ferings. Mau had tried to see novice Kinh Tam. She
asked novice Thanh Tam to pass on a message that
she wished to meet privately with novice Kinh Tam, as
she had several questions to put to him. But the young
novice asked the older novice to relay the message that
he had too many tasks in the meditation hall and did
not have time to meet with her.

Humiliated and angry, she rushed back home, not
even staying as she normally did to listen to the abbot's
teachings. Sitting on the verandah beside the tea bushes,
Mau was infuriated. She burst into tears, burying her
face in her hands. She thought of Kinh Tam, still longing for him to take her in his arms. The sky was very
clear, the moon shone so brightly, yet Mau's heart was
utterly desolate.

Suddenly Mau noticed someone standing nearby. A
shadow appeared on the moonlit courtyard. Looking
up, she recognized Thuong, her family's servant boy.
Thuong was looking at her with pity. Mau seemed to
look through Thuong, as if she was seeing the novice
instead. She raised her two arms, gesturing him to
come closer. She pulled him close to her, then led the

young servant into her bedroom. Mau was in a state of delirium, completely overtaken by the force of her sensual craving, despondency, and wounded pride.

Mau led Thuong to her bed and let nature take its course, all the while imagining she was with Kinh Tam. She passionately held the imagined novice in her arms and ardently pressed her lips to his as if possessed.

The entire episode lasted less than five minutes. Immediately afterwards, Mau lashed out at Thuong and chased him from the room. Cowering with his head in his hands, Thuong ran, realizing he had just committed a fatal mistake. He surely would be put to death if his master were to learn of this incident; and his parents living out in the countryside also would be implicated. As for Mau, in the days that followed, the girl lived in agony, full of terror and regret.

One morning, Mau woke up with a lot of physical discomfort. From various indications, she realized she was pregnant. Her fear rose to even greater heights. She worried for herself, for her parents, and also for Thuong. All four people were now to be victims of her obsession, her sensual desires, her wounded pride and her vengefulness. After confirming that she truly was pregnant, Mau made arrangements to get a large sum of money. She gave it to Thuong and told him to flee from the country, never to return, not even to his parents' home in Nhat Nam. She was well aware of her father's violent temper. He surely would make things very difficult for Thuong's parents.

Tearfully, young Thuong took the money she proffered and left that very day. Some months later, Mau's parents noticed the changes in their daughter and knew the worst had happened. They queried her for details, but Mau adamantly refused to answer. She was ashamed. She could not acknowledge the truth, even to these two who had given her life. She could not tell them she had slept with a servant boy. She herself could not accept such a deed, nor would people in their society accept it. The couple questioned their beloved daughter repeatedly for three days and three nights, but Mau just kept silent. She casually said she was just unwell, that was all. On the fourth day, while the three of them were in the front hall eating their meal, the village bailiff called for Thi Mau—the wanton young woman who had gotten pregnant out of wedlock, the daughter of the wealthiest high-class family—to present herself at the village town hall and explain her actions, after which the village council would proclaim judgment.

The rich couple was ashamed and humiliated beyond words. They had high status in the village, always having the seats of honor and being served the most delectable dishes. Upon seeing them, everyone had had to bow low and offer good wishes to them. Now their daughter had just been commanded to answer for the crime of getting pregnant out of wedlock. How would they ever be able to face anyone in the village again?

Mau's father escorted and presented her to the village council, while her mother stayed home. Looking at the father and daughter, the council chairman said, "Thi Mau, dear child, you have foolishly gotten pregnant by someone. You should say what happened for all in the village to know. If you tell the truth, then the village council will arrange for you to marry the man. However, if you should tell even a small lie, your father will not be able to redeem your actions even with a payment of nine buffaloes and thirty cows!"

The chairman looked directly at Mau, and the other members of the council studied her face closely. Mau's father also looked squarely at her. She avoided everyone's gaze by casting her own eyes downward and thought, "I cannot tell the truth. Doing so would bring utter shame to my parents, to my entire lineage. Many families of good standing offered me proposals to marry their sons. I refused them all, only to end up sleeping with a servant boy. Even if I were to tell the truth, no one would believe me, especially now that Thuong has fled. Why don't I just say I slept with novice Kinh Tam—the one I love? The council chairman promised that, according to the village's regulation, I would be wedded to Kinh Tam, if I say he is the one . . ."

As her thoughts tumbled to this point, Mau looked up at the chairman and said, "I was foolish. I slept with Kinh Tam, a novice now practicing up at Dharma Cloud Temple. I did so because I love novice Kinh Tam. I could not resist. I beg for the forgiveness of everyone in the village and for your help in marrying us."

Everyone simultaneously cried out in surprise. Incredible! How could so righteous a novice as Kinh Tam commit such a deed as this?

The chairman asked, "So where did you sleep with the novice and conceive this baby?"

Mau quickly answered, "Some months ago we sat behind the patriarch's stupa in the temple. It was near six o'clock in the evening."

The chairman turned and directed the two guards standing by, "You two, go up to the temple and bring back the venerable abbot and the novice Kinh Tam right away for some questioning by the village council."

Within an hour's time, the abbot of Dharma Cloud arrived. Novice Kinh Tam was with him. The two elder novices, Chi Tam and Thanh Tam, also came.

After inviting the venerable abbot to sit down, the chairman looked at novice Kinh Tam and asked, "Novice, you have taken the monastic vows and committed to live the celibate life of a monk. So why have you transgressed your vows in sleeping with this young maiden and getting her pregnant?"

Then the chairman pointed at Mau and continued, "Thi Mau has already given the council her full account. Novice, if you own up to your reckless deed, the council will grant mercy by allowing you to leave the monastic life and marry Thi Mau. But if you should deny it and tell lies, the council will have to decree punishment according to the village laws established since long ago."

*Chapter Five*

# UNBEARABLE INJUSTICE

Great despair surged up from the utmost depths of the novice's being. Never could Kinh Tam have imagined that such a circumstance would occur. "Not so long ago," Kinh Tam thought, "I was subjected to an outrageous case of false accusation. Now I have just become the victim of a second injustice, maybe even more intolerable." But the novice did not allow the despair to take over completely. Kinh Tam stood silently, with palms joined, eyes closed, breathing with highly focused awareness.

Then the novice looked straight ahead and calmly addressed the chairman. "Respected chairman, respected village council, I am a monk, committed to rigorously observe the monastic vows I took. How could such a transgression occur? Lord Buddha above is my witness. I, novice Kinh Tam, assert that since the day of my ordination, I have never transgressed my vow of chastity, with any person. This young woman here must have mistaken me for another person."

The words spoken by the novice were logical, clear, and solemn. The chairman turned to ask Mau to respond. In an incisively sharp tone, Mau simply repeated the story she had already given and once again kept her eyes downcast.

Novice Chi Tam was unable to restrain his furious temper. He screamed loudly, "Young lady, you should not falsely accuse my younger brother of such an offense. Six o'clock is when all three of us novices do our evening chanting. Novice Kinh Tam from his ordination till this day has never missed a period of evening chanting. How could he have been with you behind the patriarch's stupa at that time?"

Mau quickly backtracked on the point. "Maybe I did not remember the correct time. Maybe it was before the evening chanting session, between four and five o'clock in the afternoon."

Seeing how resolute Mau was, the chairman ordered, "Thi Mau has confessed, but novice Kinh Tam refuses to admit his fault. Guards! Spread him out face down on the mat and strike him seven times with the raffia pole. Let's see whether this dishonest novice will continue to deny his grave offense."

Two guards took Kinh Tam to the large straw mat in the middle of the courtyard and spread the novice's arms and legs out flat on the middle of the mat. One of the guards struck Kinh Tam repeatedly with the raffia pole, each blow sharp and hard.

Novice Chi Tam bellowed, "You will kill him, hitting him like that!" But his exclamation could not stop the guard. Although Kinh Tam took seven excruciating blows, the novice did not let out a single cry.

The abbot compassionately implored his student, "Kinh Tam, if you really were inadvertently so foolish, then you should truthfully confess to the village council. Then you can be cleansed of the wrong deed and begin anew as you continue with your monastic practice. I will try my best to gather enough money to pay the fine and compensation for you. Confess now, dear disciple, or else they will punish you with more blows that you will not be able to withstand. Your strength and stature are those of a scholar; you are not as strong as your elder brother Chi Tam."

Novice Kinh Tam joined his palms and turned toward the abbot. "Respected teacher, as I did not transgress any vows, I cannot say that I did. Please, respected teacher, be compassionate and accept my determination not to concede to this false accusation."

The chairman shouted another command for the guard to question and to strike Kinh Tam another thirty blows. Blood soaked through the novice's monastic attire. As the interrogation went on, Brother Thanh Tam could not endure any more. He sobbed out loud, covering his eyes with his two hands.

Abruptly, Thi Mau screamed. She stood up, walked toward the mat, and bellowed, "Go on hitting, keep striking the blows, and don't stop till he dies! And how about me? Strike me as well! Hit me till I also die!" Thi Mau tore at her clothes, beat her hands on her head, and pounded her chest.

Suddenly there was a loud clearing of the throat, and a baritone voice, deep as the sound of a large brass bell, boomed through the courtyard. It was the voice of the abbot of Dharma Cloud. The Zen teacher was standing and reciting a meditation verse:

*The river of attachment is thousands of miles long.*
*The waves on the ocean of suffering rise thousands*
   *of miles high.*

*To free ourselves from the realm of samsara,*
*let us invoke the Buddha's name with one-pointed*
*concentration.*

The recitation was so solemn and powerful that it caused even the guard to stop his hand and look at the Zen teacher. The entire gathering froze in place.

After finishing the recitation, the abbot calmly spoke. "Respected chairman, respected members of the village council, in this turmoil the parties involved may have some dilemma that cannot be publicly shared at this time. I implore the chairman and members of the village council to open your compassionate hearts and show mercy by allowing me to take novice Kinh Tam back to the temple for further counsel and guidance. I truly believe that novice Kinh Tam does have the deep intention to live the monastic life. Over the entire past two years, never have I witnessed the novice transgressing any monastic precepts or fine manners, however minute. I ask to serve as surety for the novice, to bring him back to the temple, and, I hope, with more time to be able to find the truth of the matter. As a monk of long standing who has dwelled at Dharma Cloud

Temple for over forty years, I beseech the village council to accept this request."

The powerful words of the abbot moved the majority of the village council to nod their heads in agreement. The chairman moved to adjourn. The council decided to postpone the dispute for an unspecified period, and neither Kinh Tam nor Thi Mau had to pay any penalty during this time.

The abbot told the two elder novices to help Kinh Tam back to the temple.

Upon return to the temple, Kinh Tam asked the elder novices to bring a large tub of hot water into the room and take their leave for the night. The two elder novices acceded to Kinh Tam's request, even though they both felt deep compassion and wanted to help treat the wounds of their dear junior monk, for whom they had much respect.

Later that evening, while lying on the bed recovering, Kinh Tam heard knocking at the door. Asking who it was, the novice heard the voice of elder brother Thanh Tam. Thanh Tam had gone down to the village and gotten some herbal medicine that speeds up the healing of wounds. Kinh Tam asked the elder brother to leave the prepared bowl of medicine in front of the door. And, since Kinh Tam was in no condition to climb up to the bell tower to do the evening chanting, the novice asked Thanh Tam to take over the task for that evening and the following days.

*Chapter Six*

# SHARPENING
# THE SWORD

Waking up the next morning, despite the inescapable physical pain, Kinh Tam felt an extremely pleasant emotion that the novice had never previously experienced. Kinh Tam felt a whole new elation.

The previous day, the novice had been deeply torn between two choices, either to reveal the truth that would prove beyond any question Kinh Tam's innocence and put an end to all suspicion and interrogation, or to go on keeping the secret in order to be able to continue the life of a monastic. The novice simply did not have the strength to withstand the force of more blows. Kinh Tam had felt excruciating pain piercing to the bone each time the large raffia pole came thundering down. The novice tried hard to endure the pain and not scream or plead for mercy.

Kinh Tam knew that revealing the truth would stop the physical abuse and correct the injustice, but also that the truth would bring an immediate end to the novice's monastic life in the temple. The happiness of living that life was so enormous that Kinh Tam just could not part with it. Better to endure extreme pain and public scorn in order to retain the delight of living as a monastic.

"They falsely accused me; they reviled me and misunderstood me. They interrogated me and then violently punished me. But staying true to my ideal and my true happiness, I was able to endure with openness and magnanimity such flagrant injustice." Lying in bed, the novice felt something like a kind of bliss. Kinh Tam realized that this lighthearted feeling of freedom was the result of the successful practice of inclusiveness, of magnanimity.

Five days later and largely recovered, Kinh Tam donned the saffron-colored ceremonial sanghati robe to prostrate in front of the abbot. Although the novice had not transgressed any vows or committed any offense, still it was because of Kinh Tam that this respected Zen teacher had to bear the brunt of many bad rumors. After the novice finished prostratiing and folded up the sanghati robe, the abbot told his young disciple to sit down. The two older novices were also present.

"According to the news your two elder brothers have presented, there's been quite a commotion about this incident in the village. Only a few people seem to have any understanding or compassion for you. The majority of the villagers tend to believe Mau's testimony. Everyone is talking about the charge and making a real mockery of it. We are in a grievous situation. You must be very careful, Kinh Tam."

Novice Chi Tam joined his palms. "Respected teacher, those who understand and believe in us are the people who come regularly to hear the teachings and help out around the temple, and so had more interactions with you and with us novices. They are practicing the lay precept against speaking untruthfully, and although they have yet to understand the circumstances and may not fully believe that Kinh Tam is completely innocent, they have steadfastly refrained from ridiculing or saying anything disrespectful. Of course, the imprudent people are many. They have a penchant for listening to gossip and spreading rumors. There are those who question why the abbot has not already expelled novice Kinh Tam instead of allowing a person who transgressed his vows to continue to live in the temple. Dear respected teacher, it is true that our community is meeting with misfortune. I see that the three of us novices must do the practice of acknowledging our faults and beginning anew daily, to connect with the limitless wisdom of loving-kindness, compassion, joy, and equanimity to strengthen our endurance and rise above this calamity."

The abbot looked at novice Kinh Tam. "Your elder brother's suggestion is apt. Though you are innocent and never transgressed your vows, you should still do the practice of acknowledging faults and beginning anew daily. I will also join you in doing the practice of beginning anew, my disciples. We will practice in order to completely cleanse all remnants of past unwholesome karmic actions, to renew our whole being and all our actions. I do not expect any of my disciples to be perfect or never make mistakes. No, my disciples; you, and I as well, we are not yet noble beings. I only require of you one thing: once you have committed an error, you need to learn the lessons it holds for you, so that you never commit it a second time. As long as you can do that, I will always be standing by you and supporting you, whether I am alive or have already passed away."

Deeply moved by the abbot's compassionate words, all three novices stood up and prostrated three times in gratitude to their beloved teacher.

Later that evening, after the chanting session, Kinh Tam again came to prostrate before the abbot and asked for permission to put up a temporary thatched hut just outside the temple gates to dwell in. Kinh Tam explained that this might help reduce the derisiveness of the villagers' wagging tongues aimed at the abbot and the temple. At first the abbot demurred, but finally he relented after seeing that Kinh Tam was so eager and sincere about the request.

He advised, "You are my disciple, my spiritual child, and I have faith in you. I trust you to practice diligently in order to overcome your sorrows and the internal wounds of injustice. Whether or not you have erred, you are still my spiritual child, still my continuation. And I will do all I can to support you on your path of practice."

Over the next few weeks, Kinh Tam labored with the two elder novices to build the thatched hut. During those days, a new aspirant arrived at the temple. The abbot accepted the request of Man, a seven-year-old boy, to live in the temple and become a student. Man was the son of Bac Hang, a fisherman of the next village. Man had been motherless since the age of three. Man was allowed to have his hair shaved off, except for a small patch on top, and to wear the nhat binh monastic robe. The little boy looked very quaint in that outfit. Man began to study and memorize the two daily chanting texts and to help the novices with the everyday tasks in the garden and the kitchen.

The thatched hut built by the novices was completed at last. It was outside the gates, but still on temple land. Although Kinh Tam lived in the hut, the novice was allowed to come into the temple and participate with the teacher and elder brothers in all chanting and beginning anew practices as well as working around the temple. It was still Kinh Tam's duty to ring the great bell every evening. The two elder brothers were very surprised when they neither saw any sadness on the novice's face nor heard any words of reproach toward anyone, even though people continued to slander and revile Kinh Tam. In a discussion on the practice, Thanh Tam asked Kinh Tam how the young novice was able to maintain such carefree and tranquil composure.

Kinh Tam answered, "It is because I have learned and am applying the practice of inclusiveness that I am able to avoid falling into suffering and reproach. Practicing magnanimity brings us away from the shore of sorrows and over to the shore of freedom and happiness. *Paramita,* as my elder brothers already know, means 'crossing over to the other shore.' According to *The Collection on the Six Paramitas,* the Buddha taught:

*Those who are caught in cravings*
*are no longer clear-minded,*
*which causes them to inflict pain and humiliation*
   *on us.*
*If we are able to magnanimously persevere,*
*then our hearts and minds will be at peace.*
*Those who are self-indulgent*
*do not abide by moral conduct,*
*which causes them to slander and harm us.*
*If we are able to magnanimously persevere,*
*then our hearts and minds will be at peace.*
*Those who are ungrateful tell lies about us.*
*The gardens of their minds are full of the weeds of*
   *vengeance,*
*which causes them to treat us unfairly and unjustly.*
*If we are able to magnanimously persevere,*
*then our hearts and minds will be at peace."*

Kinh Tam then quoted a section from a sutra in which the Buddha talks about putting a handful of salt into a small bowl of water. That bowl of water will be too salty for a thirsty person to drink. If, however, one were to toss that same handful of salt into a river, the situation would be completely different. Although the amount of salt is the same, it cannot cause the river to become too salty, because the river is so immense and the water is in constant flux, day and night. Anyone taking a drink from the river would find freshwater and not be bothered by the addition of a handful of salt.

The novice continued to share. "When we truly practice looking deeply, then we have a chance to understand better and to be more accepting. Our hearts naturally open up, becoming vast like the oceans and rivers. In understanding the sorrows and difficulties of others, we are able to accept and feel compassion for them, even if they have caused us difficulties, treated us unfairly, brought disaster upon us, or unjustly harassed us. Due to desire, vengeance, ignorance, and jealousy, people have made numerous mistakes and caused much suffering to themselves and others. If we can comprehend this, then we will no longer condemn or resent others. As we become more inclusive, our hearts and minds will be at peace."

In closing, novice Kinh Tam continued, "Being magnanimous does not mean suppressing suffering, nor does it mean gritting our teeth and bearing things with resentment or even resignation. These reactions are not inclusiveness or magnanimity (*kshanti paramita*) and cannot take us over to the other shore. We must practice deep looking and contemplation in order to understand and cultivate loving-kindness, compassion, joy, and equanimity. In cultivating loving-kindness, we offer happiness; in nurturing compassion, we relieve others' suffering; practicing diligently strengthens our inner source of joy; and developing equanimity helps us let go of all hatred, prejudices, and entanglements. When our heart is filled with loving-kindness, compassion, joy, and equanimity, its capacity becomes boundless, immeasurable. With such an expansive heart, immense as the wide-open sea, those blatant injustices and suffering cannot overpower us, just as a small handful of salt cannot make a great river salty. Because I have been able to learn and apply the practice of these Four Immeasurable Minds, I can continue to live, to go deeper into the practice, and to find happiness in the life of a monk."

Listening to Kinh Tam's statements, the elder novices had much admiration and happiness for their younger brother. Novice Chi Tam went the next morning and related their conversation to the abbot, who was also very pleased.

The sneering in the village over the scandal eventually quieted down—that is, until Mau completed the term of her pregnancy and gave birth to the child. In a fit of anger, Mau's father declared that Mau should take the baby to the person to whom it belonged, as he could not accept the presence of an out-of-wedlock child in his home. Still, Mau dared not reveal the truth. She didn't know what she should do. In the end, she audaciously took the newborn child to the temple and left it in the care of novice Kinh Tam.

*Chapter Seven*

# DIAMOND HEART

K inh Tam had already thought of ways to answer the abbot and the elder novices about taking in the abandoned newborn. The young novice pleaded with the elder novices for their understanding and acceptance.

These words, however, did not prevent Thanh Tam from flying into a rage and refusing to acknowledge Kinh Tam's presence for several days. This was not because Thanh Tam didn't care for Kinh Tam, but simply because he didn't fully understand. His logic was that Kinh Tam was not the child's father and so should not take on the responsibility of raising the child. Kinh Tam had barely escaped the noose of injustice, so why should the novice have to voluntarily put his own neck back into it again?

Though Thanh Tam had listened to the reasoning that "the merit of building an elaborate temple nine stories high cannot compare to that of saving the life of one person," he just could not accept it. "Why not save any other person, instead of saving *that particular* person?"

But Kinh Tam was very firm, even harder than a rock, in fact, for the novice's heart had become like a diamond. No one could stop Kinh Tam from doing what the novice believed was right. How could someone so gentle, sweet, and devoted be so stubborn? Yet within a week, Kinh Tam's steady patience helped change Thanh Tam's point of view.

Elder brother Chi Tam also disagreed at first, but he kept silent and did not show any outward signs of protest. It could be that this elder brother was pulled between two forces inside: on the one hand, his fear of people's contempt, and on the other, his faith in his younger brother, whose character was truly exceptional.

Most mysterious of all was the attitude of their teacher. After listening to Kinh Tam's sincere request, the abbot just stayed quiet. Then he said, "You have my permission to make your own arrangements. You have gained maturity and insight. Just do what you believe to be appropriate."

Raising a child was no small task. Luckily, although Aunt Han in the village did not have milk in abundance, she was still willing to share a bit for little Thien Tai. Kinh Tam had named the adopted child Thien Tai ("Good Inheritance") and called him Tai for short. The novice chewed rice down to a paste before feeding it to the little one and sang lullabies to the child using only meditations from the sutras and scriptures.

Brother Thanh Tam often helped take care of Tai. He loved to chant "Sound of the Rising Tides":

*The Universal Dharma door is open,*
*the sound of the rising tide is clear, and the miracle*
    *happens:*
*a beautiful child appears in the heart of a lotus*
    *flower!*
*A single drop of the compassionate water is enough*
*to bring back the refreshing spring to mountains*
    *and rivers.*

The new aspirant, Man, also really enjoyed cuddling baby Tai. Quite often, Man would run out to the thatched hut and ask permission to hold the baby or at least be allowed to sit beside him and watch him sleep. With the presence of little Tai, life within the temple became more cheerful. Kinh Tam raised Thien Tai with love, and the work of raising a child became a meditation practice in itself.

Since the day Kinh Tam took in the baby, elder brother Thanh Tam had been overseeing the task of sounding the large bell in the tower every evening, as Kinh Tam had asked him to do. It was quite awkward to ring the bell while carrying the child in one arm. Furthermore, the sound of the large bell was too loud, often startling the baby and making him cry. Whenever Kinh Tam missed sounding the bell too much, his elder brother would hold the baby while the novice went up to ring the bell and recite the gathas. Man also often asked permission to hold little Tai while Kinh Tam rang the bell and recited the gathas. Everyone appreciated hearing Kinh Tam's recitation. Not hearing those recitations often left them feeling something was amiss.

Quite skillful in sewing and mending, the novice made tiny monk outfits for little Tai, using only simple brown fabrics. When the little one was two years old, he was taught to call the novice "father-teacher."

As Thien Tai grew older, strangely enough, he didn't look anything like Mau, and in fact his face increasingly resembled that of his "father-teacher." This made novice Kinh Tam's conduct more suspect. No one could imagine the possibility that the seeds of virtue and diligent practice in Kinh Tam, now sown and cultivated in Thien Tai, could manifest more visibly in the child's countenance than hereditary seeds transmitted by biological parents.

Novice Chi Tam, now fully ordained and therefore called Thay Chi Tam, or Venerable Chi Tam, was considered the disciple with most seniority in years of practice at the temple and a very diligent monk. Yet even he had to admit that his diligence in the practice paled in comparison to that of the younger novice Kinh Tam. In truth, Kinh Tam had put all his energy into practicing meditation. Every evening Kinh Tam would do sitting meditation till midnight. Each time Chi Tam happened to look out toward the pine forest in front of the temple gates, he'd see the light of a kerosene lamp shining out from within Kinh Tam's thatched hut. Kinh Tam participated in all activities of the temple and was only absent when ill. Thay Chi Tam often witnessed the novice taking peaceful, relaxed, and stable steps in meditation along the dirt path in front of the temple gates. There were times when Thay Chi Tam was ashamed for not putting as much effort into his practice and studies as his younger novice brother did.

Novice Kinh Tam saw little Tai as a major subject for deeper meditation. Thien Tai was the child of Mau, yes, but also the child of Kinh Tam. This was the meditation that Kinh Tam steadfastly focused on.

During these periods of meditation, Kinh Tam thought deeply about all the scandals, injustices, and suffering that had transpired. The novice would think deeply about all the individuals directly involved to gain further insight and clarity. Kinh Tam always started with self-directed personal reflection.

The second focus was Thien Si. It seemed Thien Si was trapped. The only son of a rich family, he had many advantages for acquiring a good education and a successful career, but the young man just could not be master of his own life. Thien Si was living as a shadow of his parents, completely under their control, just like a marionette moving under the puppeteer's strings. He was not capable of making his own judgments about things or of creating happiness for himself and his beloved.

Kinh Tam thought back to the critical moment of the accusation of attempted murder. Thien Si was sitting there, wanting to say something, but he was ultimately unable to voice his thoughts. He was about to lose his wife, yet he could not take charge of the situation or even make any decision at all. His parents resolved to send their daughter-in-law away. How could he oppose them? Kinh had tried to change the situation, but could not. In returning home Kinh had felt quite light in heart and mind, not holding any grudge toward Thien Si. At the same time, Kinh did not have much respect for him, and without respect, marital love simply could not survive.

The third subject of this meditation was Mau. Daughter of a rich family, she had beauty and position, but not happiness. Although her suitors were numerous, she had never been truly loved. Even the young man whom Mau had bedded she neither loved nor respected. The novice did not need to know who that man was. What the novice knew with certainty was that Mau did not love that person. Both Mau and that man were simply victims of the raging fires of passion.

Mau fell in love, but fatally, as that love came up against two major obstacles. The first was that the person she loved had taken monastic vows. The second was that the person she loved was a young woman in disguise. Furthermore, Mau did not know how to practice in accord with the teachings of the Buddha, such as the Five Mindfulness Trainings (Buddhist precepts). No one had helped Mau understand that body and mind are like deep oceans containing dark, hidden whirlpools and sea monsters that can capsize the boat of our life in seconds. When one is miserable, lonely, and hopeless because of an impossible love, wealth or beauty has no real value. The issue is how to actually create happiness.

Both Kinh Tam and Mau were in danger of being drowned in the ocean of suffering and ignorance. If Kinh Tam had not practiced, the novice would not have been able to escape that ocean. Mau had hoped to trap Kinh Tam into admitting to the alleged tryst. The young woman still had confidence in the strength of her influence, her power, and her position in society. But Kinh Tam had defied all of that. Mau's pride and conceit were totally demolished. It could be said that she suffered the most. What was left for her to feel happy about in life? Could it be that the only path remaining for her was the path of practice?

The fourth person was the biological father of
Thien Tai. Whether that man was rich or poor, young
or old, of high or low social class, acquainted with the
novice or not, still living in the village or long gone
away to another place, all was of little importance to
the novice. Kinh Tam only saw that the man also suffered greatly. He had suffered because Mau did not
acknowledge him, even though she had allowed him
to be physically intimate with her. If Mau had loved
him, she would have reported his name to the village
council and had their wedding arranged. The truth
was that Mau did not love him, and she was afraid of
even mentioning his name. Clearly, he was also terrified and dared not make himself known or publicly
acknowledge his son. Perhaps he didn't even know he
had a child at all. He would not have been caught in
this web and forced to go into hiding if Mau hadn't
been obsessed, desperate, and miserable. The man had
also fallen victim to ignorance and fear. Would he ever
escape his predicament?

Of the four, only Kinh Tam was able to see the way
out and had been able to practice so as not to be overwhelmed by the grave injustices that occurred. Looking

around, the novice saw that numerous other young people were also caught in conditions of suffering similar to the situation of these four. How many had been able, as the novice had been, to find a path to escape misery and be truly free?

Kinh Tam's heart and spirit felt light and free thanks to this practice of looking deeply to bring forth the energies of loving-kindness and compassion from within, like freshwater springing up from deep inside the Earth. Looking at the other three, Thien Si, Mau, and little Thien Tai's father, the novice saw each one had suffered; each was still struggling to navigate the boat of life over the turbulent seas of ignorance and desires, getting tossed around by the waves, and often going under. With this understanding, Kinh Tam was able to truly love these three people. Now filled with compassion, the novice's heart was free from hatred, resentment, and hurt. Kinh Tam knew that more practice would be necessary to one day help the three, and others, to find their own understanding and be released from their suffering.

The novice surmised, "How heart-wrenching it is to see young people continuing to go down such painful paths. My father, my mother, my teacher, my elder novice brothers, and even little Thien Tai were also victims and had to bear some of the consequences, although none of them was responsible for any part of the suffering or misdeeds."

*Chapter Eight*

# GREAT VOW

Surely anyone who has lived on Earth has had to experience injustice of one kind or another. If we allow hatred and revenge to dictate our response, then our suffering will only go on and on. How do we find a way out? How can we free ourselves? A person who feels injured by another typically harbors thoughts of revenge, wanting to punish the offender. But the Buddha taught that hatred is never removed by adding more hatred. The only stream that can wash away the pain of unjust acts is the sweet water of loving-kindness and compassion. Without loving-kindness and compassion, hatred and vengeance will continue to accumulate from one year, and one lifetime, to the next.

It was while mindfully going about daily activities such as sitting and walking meditation, preparing vegetables or fetching water from the well that novice Kinh Tam had used the powerful sword of insight meditation to cut through afflictions, suffering, and grievances. The novice's mind and heart were now truly peaceful, happy, and free.

Months and years had passed. Thien Tai was now six years old. Aspirant Man was thirteen and had already officially taken the novice vows with the Dharma name Man Tam ("Heart of Fulfillment"). The previous year Brother Thanh Tam received the full ordination vows at a ceremony organized in the mountain district of Long Bien.

Novice Kinh Tam had asked to be permitted, after receiving the full vows, to visit home. Back at home, younger brother Chau was now twenty-five years old. He might already have finished studying at Dai Tap University, and might even have been selected for and taken one examination as well. Kinh Tam had been practicing at Dharma Cloud Temple for over eight years and during that time never had dared to write a single letter home.

Unfortunately, Kinh Tam fell ill before the full-vows ordination ceremony. Although very sick with pneumonia, the novice refused to allow any healers inside the thatched hut for diagnosis. For ten days straight, Kinh Tam was not able to swallow anything, not even rice broth. Little Tai, though still so very young, knew enough to worry about his father-teacher's health.

Thien Tai was quite bright. He had memorized many sutras and gathas without having to formally study them. He already knew how to do sitting and walking meditation and could help novice Man Tam with cleaning tasks and preparing vegetables. During his father-teacher's illness, the little aspirant hung around the thatched hut doing small jobs like boiling water, getting fresh ginger from the temple, and going to find Thay Thanh Tam to do something for his father-teacher. Thien Tai was old enough now to be sleeping every night in the temple, in novice Man Tam's room.

Kinh Tam had a high fever for many nights and was now often coughing up a great deal of blood. Late one evening, after the fever had gone down, Kinh Tam knew death was near. The novice sat up. Outside, the full moon was shining brightly. Kinh Tam drew her last bit of strength together to write letters to the abbot and to her parents.

Kinh Tam felt remarkably peaceful; and in thinking of her parents, her brother Chau, and her elder Dharma brothers, the novice suddenly felt an inner boost of energy that allowed her to write three letters in a row. The first letter was to her parents and her brother, the second to the abbot her teacher, and the third to Mau. The novice's hand did not tremble one bit while writing with the ink brush.

In her letter to the abbot, the novice first asked for forgiveness for her deception in disguising herself as a man. Her only defense was that the wish to practice as a monastic was too great for her to overcome. The novice shared about everything in her heart, including her dream of seeing the establishment of a temple where women could practice the monastic life. She also asked permission to have her elder Dharma brother Chi Tam travel all the way to Cuu Chan district to hand-deliver a letter she had written to her parents, and to allow aspirant Thien Tai also to go along and be presented to his grandparents. Kinh Tam carefully noted her parents' full names and address, including village, district, and region. Last, the novice offered the abbot nine prostrations to express her faith and infinite gratitude to the teacher for whom she had utmost respect and love. The novice averred that the abbot had opened the spiritual path for her, and that all she had attained in the practice was entirely due to the abbot's insights, loving-kindness, and compassion. In closing, the novice urgently entreated the abbot to find ways to realize her deepest last wish, which was to establish a temple for nuns.

In the letter to her parents, after she apologized for her actions lacking in filial piety and explained the reasons that had brought her to live a monastic life, Kinh Tam shared with her parents the tremendous happiness she had known throughout her time living as a monastic. She also recounted, in a light and charming manner, the incident involving her and a young woman in the village. The novice thanked Chau for taking care of their parents in her stead during the last eight years, and gratefully acknowledged that she had been able to succeed on the path of practice due in large part to him. Kinh Tam asked her parents to inform her husband, Thien Si, and invite him to come along with them when they traveled to Giao Chi district for her funeral and cremation services. She also spoke about the practice of inclusiveness, and the peace and happiness gained from wholehearted spiritual practice. In closing, the novice expressed her hope that her parents would regard aspirant Thien Tai as their grandson.

In her letter to Mau, after telling about her life, the novice said that she did not hold any grudge toward

Mau at all; she knew Mau had been driven by despair, and this was why the novice greatly hoped that Mau would diligently practice to transform all of her afflictions. Kinh Tam said she always regarded Mau as a friend and she would be very gratified if Mau were to also aspire one day to live the monastic life.

After she finished writing the letter to Mau, Kinh Tam felt completely drained. The novice released the ink brush, blew out the kerosene lamp, and, straightening her posture, began to nourish her body through the meditation exercises on breathing. Once her body and mind became calm and peaceful, Kinh Tam immediately entered the Concentration of Immeasurable Loving-kindness. Having reached potent levels of loving-kindness concentration, the novice went on into the Concentration of Immeasurable. Compassion. When she had attained full realization of this concentration, she entered the Concentration of Immeasurable Joy. A blissful smile bloomed continuously on the serene face of the novice. With full strength from the Concentration of Immeasurable Joy in her, Kinh Tam entered into the Concentration of Immeasurable Equanimity. In this concentration, loving-kindness, compassion, and joy embraced the novice and every being in the world;

there was no discrimination between loved ones and enemies. The novice opened her heart fully to all beings. She concentrated her complete mindfulness on her parents, her brother, her teacher, her elder Dharma brothers, and every single person who had supported her in the entire twenty-eight years of this life. Then with a smile, she let go of that body and life. Stably seated in the lotus position, Kinh Tam passed away.

The next morning, it was little aspirant Thien Tai who went out to the thatched hut quite early and found that his father-teacher had just died. In a panic, he ran to find novice Man Tam. As Man Tam went looking for Thay Thanh Tam, Thay Chi Tam was already approaching the hermitage of Kinh Tam and also saw that his younger Dharma brother had passed away, in the lotus position, on the bamboo bed inside the hut. He had just lowered the corpse down to a lying position when Thay Thanh Tam arrived. Within minutes, the two venerables discovered that their younger Dharma brother Kinh Tam was a woman.

Thay Chi Tam told everyone present to step out of the hut and instructed all to join their palms while invoking the Buddha's name. He was crying as he went back through the temple gates to find the abbot, who was also moved to tears upon hearing the news. The abbot instructed Thay Chi Tam to go down to the village to relay the news to the village council chairman and other members of the council. He also told him to invite several laywomen practitioners living near the temple to come up and help with the preparation of the body of novice Kinh Tam for the funeral and cremation.

*Chapter Nine*

# LOVING
# HEART

News that novice Kinh Tam was a woman flashed like lightning throughout all the villages in the district. People from the village just below and various other nearby villages continually thronged around Dharma Cloud Temple. Lay Buddhists, youths, elders, steadfast supporters, erstwhile accusers—everyone was greatly moved. By noon, the temple grounds were packed full.

The abbot had read novice Kinh Tam's letter to him and immediately gave permission for Venerable Chi Tam to go to Kinh Tam's home village, to take little Thien Tai to be presented, and to hand-deliver the letter that Kinh Tam had written to her parents. The abbot also told novice Man Tam to deliver Kinh Tam's letter to Thi Mau in the village below. Thi Mau was not home when the little novice came to her house. In fact, she had already heard the news and had gone up to the temple two hours earlier. Novice Man Tam had to return to the temple and, after a long search, finally found Thi Mau and gave her the letter.

The corpse of Kinh Tam was moved to the West Hall, which was brightly lit with numerous candles and richly perfumed with incense day and night. The abbot himself presided over all the chanting and praying sessions, only to be replaced by Thay Thanh Tam when the abbot got tired. The chanting echoed clearly out to the outer courtyards of the temple. So many people shed so many tears. They commented to each other, "Practicing like that is really true practice. Being able to peacefully endure things so difficult to endure is truly the practice of magnanimity—*kshanti paramita*. How horrible, the way Kinh Tam was treated for over six years!" Many of the men present were red-eyed, while women shamelessly sobbed and cried out loud. The chanting ceaselessly rolled out over and above all the commotion.

The casket of novice Kinh Tam was to be displayed for seven days in the West Hall before being moved to the funeral pyre in front of the temple gate, exactly on the spot of the thatched hut of the novice. Thay Chi Tam was given permission to travel on horseback in order to bring Kinh Tam's family back in time for the cremation services. The family of Thi Mau presented itself to the village council, requesting to bear all funeral costs. All members of this upper-class family heeded the advice of the abbot and came to stay in the humble accommodations at the temple for those seven days. They ate simple vegetarian meals, slept on the ground with modest bedding, read sutras, chanted texts of repentance and beginning anew, and prayed.

Mau cried herself dry. During the ceremony to receive mourning cloths, she had knelt down and asked to receive the mourning cloth of a blood sister of the novice. A marked change had come over Thi Mau. Ever since hearing the truth and then receiving the mourning cloth, her face and indeed her entire physical appearance had become completely different. All signs of melancholy and despair vanished. Her face shone brightly like that of a person who had found someone who truly loved her. Under the instruction of the abbot, copies of *The Collection on the Six Paramitas* collated by Master Tang Hoi were distributed for constant chanting day and night. Everyone eventually memorized the gathas on the teaching on magnanimity.

Finally Venerable Chi Tam returned. He announced that a two-horse coach was arriving shortly, carrying Kinh Tam's parents Mr. and Mrs. Ly, Chau, Thien Si, and little Thien Tai. He relayed that Thien Tai had been fully accepted as a blood grandchild by Kinh

Tam's parents, who naturally had cried in reading the letter Kinh Tam had written to them. Eight long years they had searched and waited in vain for news of their beloved daughter, and now, when they finally received news, it was of her demise.

The coach stopped at the foot of the hills. Looking up toward the temple, Mr. and Mrs. Ly saw the red banner fluttering in the wind bearing the Dharma name of novice Kinh Tam and burst into tears once again. The cremation ceremony was planned to begin exactly at noon, but already the temple grounds were packed full with over three thousand people. The chanting continued to echo out to the outer courtyards of the temple. A bridge made out of white silk hundreds of meters long was put up to represent the path or bridge from the shore of suffering to the shore of freedom.

The abbot himself went out to greet and receive the Ly family and Thien Si. He ushered them into his quarters to comfort them in their grief, led them in to pay homage to the Buddha, and finally brought them to the West Hall to pay respects to their beloved, the novice Kinh Tam. The deceased novice's facial expression was quite tranquil; there was still a trace of the smile from the moment of last release. Everyone knelt down in front of the altar to receive their respective mourning cloths: Chau as younger brother of the novice, Thien Si as husband, and Thien Tai as Dharma son. Everyone made the solemn vow to practice in accord with the Five Mindfulness Trainings and to diligently practice invoking the Buddha's names and chanting the sutras.

Great rolling sounds of the giant bell and thundering rhythms of the drum announced the time to close the casket and start the procession to the funeral pyre. The crowd of devotees was told to make way. The Ly elders, Mau's parents, Chau, Thien Si, Mau, and little Thien Tai wore their mourning cloths and walked behind the coffin. The Venerables Chi Tam and Thanh Tam headed the ceremony, leading everyone in the invocation and chanting of the sutras. Sandalwood incense permeated the air, its perfume helping everyone present to open up their hearts and embrace the entire cosmos. The deep, slow sounds of the giant bell, deliberately unhurried, gently coaxed people to release all tension and be at peace.

At this moment, there was not a single person in the crowd whose heart held any hatred or division. At this moment, there was not a single person in the crowd still harboring any bitterness or vindictiveness. Over three thousand people were present, yet every single person's heart was infused with the energy of true love. The heart of novice Kinh Tam had entered into the hearts of all the people. Kinh Tam was distinctly present in this earthly world, as well as on the shore of true freedom.

As flames consumed the pyre, the abbot, in ceremonial robes, pointed up at an unusually bright patch in the sky. Everyone looked up. Many saw a large area of multicolored clouds—a highly auspicious sign according to tradition. Novice Kinh Tam was a true practitioner; it was evident that she had succeeded in attaining full liberation.

It was two o'clock when the fire finally died out. The Venerables Chi Tam and Thanh Tam instructed devotees to sprinkle perfumed water over the hot embers and to gather the ashes of Kinh Tam. They found in the collected ashes seventy-five relics. Some relics were the size of the knuckle of a little finger, shining like pearls, while others were the size of sesame seeds, all shimmering with the auspicious combination of five colors. The two monks gathered the relics into a white ceramic urn, to be put on the altar in the temple for veneration.

Standing on a high dais, the abbot began teaching the Dharma to the large audience. Although he was nearly seventy years old, his voice was as powerful and commanding as the sound of the great bell. He declared that although Kinh Tam was a novice and had not taken full vows, she had succeeded in the practice and gained full enlightenment. The novice was truly the manifestation of a great being. Kinh Tam's full commitment to personally living a magnanimous life proved that the novice was already a true sage. Kinh Tam's heart had become a boundless heart of loving-kindness, compassion, joy, and equanimity, with the capacity to embrace every living being.

The abbot paused and then continued with a new air of reverence as he told the story of a visitation. In the abbot's sitting meditation the night before, the Buddha had appeared, holding a lotus flower in his left hand and making the great auspicious mudra gesture with his right. The Buddha told the abbot that Kinh Tam had achieved the highest attainment of a bodhisattva and was now peacefully abiding in the Dharma Cloud Realm. A beam of bright light shone forth from the little finger of the World-Honored One's right hand, still in the position of the auspicious mudra. Looking up at the sky in the direction indicated by the beam of light, the abbot had seen a magnificently jeweled lotus dais with a thousand petals. Sitting on the lotus dais was a bodhisattva whose bearing was extremely upright and whose facial features were exactly those of novice Kinh Tam. The bodhisattva had smiled and joined her palms in respect toward the abbot, who in turn joined his palms respectfully as his heart overflowed with serene joy and admiration. Interestingly, the abbot also saw the little aspirant Thien Tai standing with palms joined behind the bodhisattva's lotus dais. Although the apparition lasted only very briefly, the communication was quite deep and clear. At that precise moment, an extraordinary and wondrous fragrance pervaded the abbot's room that he had never sensed before.

The abbot went on to publicly announce to the congregation that he was committed to begin building a temple where women could be ordained and practice as nuns, as Bodhisattva Kinh Tam had implored in her letter. This bodhisattva had practiced to full realization and was able to help her parents and many other people, whether closely related or not, to transcend their suffering and renew their lives. The relics of Bodhisattva Kinh Tam were to be enshrined in this temple where she had lived and practiced. The abbot went on to say that, although he was Kinh Tam's teacher, he himself had gained many insights in observing the practice of the bodhisattva. In this way, the great attainment of one practitioner benefits countless other people. He then counseled everyone present to invoke the name of the bodhisattva: "Homage to the Bodhisattva of Deep Listening Kinh Tam, Limitless Loving-kindness and Compassion, Limitless Joy and Equanimity, Limitless Magnanimity." Wholeheartedly, reverently, everyone chanted the invocation a hundred and eight times. The abbot also advised all to immediately invoke the bodhisattva's name anytime they felt irritated, angry, hurt, or aggrieved. With single-minded concentration, those afflictions would be transformed within minutes of invocation.

Then the abbot concluded the talk by reading an excerpt from a sutra in which the Buddha teaches novice Rahula about ways to deal with various situations in life. At that time, Rahula had reached the age of seventeen and was capable of receiving deeper teachings. The Buddha taught:

*Rahula, you should learn from the Earth. Whether people spread pure and fragrant flowers, freshwater, and sweet milk on the Earth or discard onto it things*

*of filth and stench like blood, pus, urine, and garbage,
the Earth quietly receives everything without feelings
of pride, attachment, grievance, or being humiliated.
Why? Because the Earth has immense embracing
capacity and has the ability to receive and transform
whatever it takes in. If your heart-mind, my dear disciple, is boundlessly immense like the Earth, then you
will also have the ability to receive and transform all
injustices and grievances. And you will no longer feel
humiliated or suffer because of them.*

*Rahula, you should learn from water. Whether
people throw into water things which are pure and
pleasant or wash in it things of filth and stench,
water quietly receives everything without feelings of
pride, attachment, grievance, or being humiliated.
Why? Because water has immense embracing
capacity, is ever-flowing, and has the ability to
receive and transform whatever it takes in. If your
heart-mind, my dear disciple, is boundlessly immense
like water, then you too will have the ability to
receive and transform all injustices and grievances.
And you will no longer feel humiliated or suffer
because of them.*

*Rahula, you should learn from fire. Fire has the ability to receive and burn all things, including things of filth and stench, without grievance or feeling humiliated. Why? Because fire has immense receptivity and the ability to burn and transform whatever people bring to it. If your heart-mind, my dear disciple, is unprejudiced and vast like fire, then you too will have the ability to receive and transform all injustices and grievances. Then your inner happiness and peace will remain unaffected by them.*

*Rahula, you should learn from air. Air has the ability to receive, carry away, and transform all odors, sweet or foul, without pride, attachment, grievance, or feeling humiliated. Why? Because air has immense embracing capacity and has the extraordinary faculty of mobility. If your heart-mind, my dear disciple, is boundlessly immense, if your heart-mind has the ability to transform and has great mobility like the air, then you too will have the ability to receive and transform all injustice and grievances people may fling at you. Then your inner happiness and peace will remain unaffected by them.*

The teachings read by the abbot were similar to the ones poetically condensed in the verses that novice Kinh Tam often chanted in early mornings and late evenings while sounding the large temple bell. The words were like drops of Dharma nectar refreshing all the listeners' hearts. Chau, Kinh Tam's younger brother, after hearing the sutra, knelt down at the abbot's feet and requested to be ordained and practice as a monk in Dharma Cloud Temple. Thien Si too knelt down at his feet and requested to be ordained. Thi Mau also came over to kneel at the abbot's feet. She affirmed to the abbot that as soon as the first temple for nuns was established, she would request to be ordained and practice there. The parents of Thi Mau and the parents of Bodhisattva Kinh Tam all knelt down, declaring their aspiration to receive and practice the Five Mindfulness Trainings. They would also wholeheartedly support the abbot in the effort to set up the first temple for nuns in the country of Giao Chau.

Dharma Cloud Temple, also known as Cloud Temple or Mulberry Temple, is the site now marking the legend of the Bodhisattva of Deep Listening Kinh Tam. And to preserve in people's memory that the bodhisattva appeared as a young woman, the local people invoke, "Homage to the Bodhisattva of Deep Listening Thi Kinh." (The middle name "Thi" is regularly given to women.) Let us happily join the people in respectfully reciting, "Homage to the Bodhisattva of Deep Listening Thi Kinh."

The End

# A BRIEF NOTE ON THE LEGEND OF QUAN AM THI KINH

A bodhisattva is a great being, an enlightened being who is animated by the desire to help all beings suffer less and enjoy peace and happiness. There are many bodhisattvas in Buddhism, each usually representing a specific virtue. Each bodhisattva may be seen as another hand of the Buddha.

A most important bodhisattva in Buddhism is Avalokiteshvara (or Avalokita), also known as Guan Yin in Chinese, Kannon in Japanese, and Quan Am (or Quan The Am) in Vietnamese. Quan Am is the Buddha's hand of love and understanding. The words *quan am* in Vietnamese mean to observe or listen deeply to the sounds or cries of the world. Quan Am has the capacity to listen to the suffering of people, to understand, and to find those people in pain and help them.

Quan Am Thi Kinh was a real, live bodhisattva re-
nowned in Vietnam for manifesting infinite forgiveness
and endless, patient forbearance. Quan Am Thi Kinh's
life story was made into a popular folk opera centuries
ago. Later, a more erudite version was composed in the
form of a six-eight verse poem in 788 lines.

It is still not known who wrote the poem about Quan
Am Thi Kinh, but it is a well-executed work deserving
its place in the history of Vietnamese literature. The first
published version in modern Vietnamese script was by
Nguyen Van Vinh in the year 1911. As for written ver-
sions of the opera, one was printed in the native script
at the end of the nineteenth century, and all others were
written by hand. In 1966, Vu Khac Khoan published a
version in Vietnamese with the input of many operatic
artists who were in Saigon with him at the time.

# THI KINH'S LEGACY

## SISTER CHAN KHONG

*Sister Chan Khong is an expatriate Vietnamese Buddhist nun and peace activist who works closely with Thich Nhat Hanh at Plum Village and around the world.*

Every Vietnamese person knows, often from earliest childhood, the story of Quan Am Thi Kinh, a manifestation of the Bodhisattva of Great Compassion. Mothers like to tell their children the story to teach them to be strong and endure when facing great hardship.

Thay Thich Nhat Hanh (*Thay* is the respectful and also affectionate term in Vietnamese for "teacher") always tells me that Thi Kinh still exists today, alive in our own society. Many of us might find ourselves in a situation like that of Thi Kinh (Kinh Tam in Thay's story) at one time or another, to one degree or another: people unfairly attacking us, whether physically or, more commonly, verbally. How many of us know how to respond as beautifully and compassionately as Thi Kinh did?

Over his many decades of life as a monk and peace activist, Thay has been subjected to a host of grave assaults and threats—some have been attempts on his physical life, countless others more in the nature of character assassination—no less than Thi Kinh. Thay has borne it all with steadfast determination, profound understanding, and great compassion; and he seems to suffer very little. He teaches us concrete ways to touch peace and happiness in every moment—all the sweet fruits of his own practice, day in and day out, over the past sixty-seven years.

I have been a student of Thay Thich Nhat Hanh since 1959, when I was twenty-one years old. Now I am seventy-three. From my fifty-two years practicing as his student, I can attest that our teacher Thay, together with his hundreds and then thousands of other students, has served humanity all over the world, promoting peace and understanding, with a boundless love that never failed nor flagged.

The story of Thi Kinh is a popular Vietnamese folk tale hundreds of years old, but Thay wrote this book to share the story as a teaching, offering a real way of being in the world that is utterly relevant for our own time in this twenty-first century. Every day, Thich Nhat Hanh lives his life in much the same way Thi Kinh lived hers. Whenever people suspecting the worst about Thay's intentions attack him, he always maintains his faith in humanity (even that of the attackers), his gentleness, and his loving demeanor. The more I look back on the many events that have happened in the lives of Thay and his students—in the 1960s, and now again in the lives of his 379 monastic students at the Prajna (Bat Nha) Monastery in Vietnam starting in 2008—the more clearly I see how Thi Kinh's story is very much that of Thay and Thay's students.

When Vietnamese people, whether young or less young, think of Thi Kinh's story, we always have a tendency to love Thi Kinh and to hate the young woman called Mau who fell in love with a monk, had sex with another man—her own family servant—and then pretended her pregnancy was from an affair with the monk Kinh Tam, even as Kinh Tam was reviled by all and flogged nearly to death by the village authority. All our compassion goes out to the novice who self-healed the wounds from the thrashing and then proceeded to care for Mau's child until the novice's death, at which time the truth about Thi Kinh finally came out.

No one could accept a person as vain, selfish, and cruel as Mau or as weak and cowardly as Thien Si. As I myself grew up and matured through decades of brutal wars in Vietnam, I saw the collapse of moral values and the increase in corruption, violence, and depravity everywhere day by day. But anytime I complained to Thay, my teacher, about how ugly people could be, Thay always gently defused my righteous indignation. He told me it's because of people's wrong perceptions about things—seeing a "poisonous snake" in the path that really is just a piece of rope—that they react with fear and violence against each other in these horrible ways. It is not these people we need to be rid of, Thay said; it is human beings' wrong views! We must train our minds and hearts to see more deeply into the whole situation and how it came to be like that, so that rather than condemning we can accept. We train ourselves not to answer violence with violence, but rather to find a way to remove the wrong perceptions that make us suffer and hurt each other.

I remember in 1964, Thay and his students, including myself, started a movement of young people that culminated in the creation of the School of Youth for Social Service (SYSS) in Vietnam. We trained thousands of young monks, nuns, and laypeople to go out into the countryside and help peasants rebuild their villages and improve their lives in the areas of education, health, economics, and organization. Our volunteer social workers would come to a village and teach the children how to read, write, and sing. When the people in the village liked what we did, we encouraged them to build a school for the children. One family would contribute a few bamboo trees, another family would bring coconut leaves to make a roof, and so on. After a school was established, we would bring some doctors and medical students to come and help for a day or two and set up a dispensary for medicines.

So the SYSS was founded on that volunteer spirit. We didn't wait for the government to get around to helping; we just initiated the projects ourselves at the grassroots level. During the war we sponsored more than ten thousand impoverished orphans. That is how we lived our engaged Buddhism. We only wanted to bring relief to people who were sick, wounded, or needy in the war zone and to poor, struggling farmers in other areas. We helped peasants help themselves by sharing ways of taking better care of their health, improving the yields of their food crops, making handicrafts to increase household income, and educating their children; we had no political ambition.

Meanwhile, politicians in Saigon were suspicious and hostile toward us because we called on them (as well as on their opponents, the Communists) to stop the war, which was causing such immense suffering to our people. When the anti-Communist authorities in Saigon saw our success in helping so many, they feared we were becoming too popular or influential. So in May 1966, a group of masked men arrived at dusk to throw grenades into various rooms, including Thay's room, at the SYSS. The curtain in Thay's room pushed the grenade back out the window, but in any case Thay was not in his room at that time; he had been invited by Cornell University to come to the United States and had just left the day before.

In June, as we were having a meeting at SYSS, masked men again came and threw grenades at SYSS workers running away from them to hide in rooms here and there. This is when I personally witnessed the first two deaths among my friends; sixteen other people were gravely wounded in that attack. Thich Nhat Hanh was still in the United States at the time, calling for a cessation of hostilities in our country.

Of course we grieved over the deaths, but we knew that those who had ordered the murders must be caught in a wrong perception about us. At the funeral, as we stood before the corpses of our friends, with our beloved teacher physically far away but vividly present in each of our hearts, we could only respond to these terrible violent injustices by declaring that we deeply regretted their wrong perceptions about us, and we also believed they could find ways to help us alleviate the suffering of poor peasants, illiterate children, sick people, and war victims, as we had no ambition other than that. Two weeks later, eight of our social workers were kidnapped and perhaps all killed, as we never heard anything of them again.

Then on July 4, 1966, a band of masked men took five of our social workers out to a riverbank and shot them. All but one of them died; but thanks to that lone survivor, we learned that before shooting our friends one masked man did say, "We're sorry, but we are forced to kill you." At the funeral we thanked that man for saying he was sorry he was forced to kill our friends, and we asked that any who received such orders in the future please try to save us any way they could. And in fact no other killings occurred after that.

To show how wrong the belief that we were seeking political power was, our peaceful young people, whose only aim was to care for people of their country, had to accept the murders of fourteen beloved friends without uttering a single word in bitterness or anger. This behavior on our part moved the hearts of many people and may have helped the killings to stop. Silent helping hands appeared everywhere. Day by day, month after month, the number of volunteer social workers grew until it reached nearly ten thousand by 1975.

Thinking back on these tragic events, it's clear that Thich Nhat Hanh's students were following in the footsteps of Quan Am Thi Kinh, never answering violence with violence, not even verbally, because they had such a beautiful teacher who taught them how to behave exactly as Thi Kinh did. In the forty-five years since then, many other sincere and groundbreaking initiatives Thay introduced to renew Buddhism have been savagely attacked; but he continually counseled us to answer with noble silence, understanding, and compassion for those who so seriously misunderstood him and us.

We humans never seem to learn enough from our tragic past. We keep repeating the same mistakes, and we need Quan Am Thi Kinh manifestations everywhere helping us to learn to practice more patience, endurance, understanding, compassion, and inclusiveness and not to retaliate, even verbally, against those who mistreat us. In this new century and new millennium, the story of dangerous wrong perceptions and violence started up again for 379 monastics ordained by Thich Nhat Hanh who were living in Prajna (Bat Nha) Monastery in the Vietnamese highlands around Bao Loc, Lam Dong Province.

After thirty-nine years of exile, in 2005 Thay had been invited back to his homeland, where he led a three-month tour of four provinces offering retreats and other events to help people learn how to cultivate mindfulness, understanding, and compassion in their daily lives. More than half of the Vietnamese population at the time had been born while Thay was exiled outside the country. The teachings he offered were so profound and relevant, they moved 125 young women and men to want to follow Thich Nhat Hanh by becoming monastics like him right away.

The abbot of a temple in Lam Dong Province offered his property to Thay so it could be turned into a monastery for these inspired young people, and very shortly the Prajna Monastery was born. In the beginning this humble temple had a good Buddha Hall and plenty of land, but only a few tin-roof houses for people to live in. Donations from all around the world came in, and we quickly built six large residences to house the hundreds of young men and women aspiring to the monastic life as taught and lived by Thay. Even though the new buildings were large, our monks and nuns slept sixteen to a room. We also built a huge meditation hall to accommodate the thousands of other people who would come to hear Thay speak.

The practice of these young people inspired others who also wished to live such a beautiful and happy simple life. By the end of 2006 there were 267 monastics residing and training at Prajna Monastery; in 2007 there were 357, and by August 2008 the number had increased to 379. They lived and served their community together joyfully, offering many humanitarian services to poor and hungry children in the area. Projects included setting up homes for children in remote villages of the region and seeing that thousands of preschool-age children were cared for, educated, and given a simple meal while their parents worked all day long as manual laborers, mostly picking tea or coffee.

Once again, the success of such a dynamic movement of talented and educated young people scared the regime. Most temples around Vietnam were lucky to ordain two or three monastics in a year. How could that old monk Thich Nhat Hanh have gotten up to several hundred monastic disciples in just three and a half years? (Besides the monks and nuns at Prajna, there were another 118 in Hue City at Thay's home temple Tu Hieu; 116 at Plum Village in France, where Thay resides; 20 at Thay's new European Institute of Applied Buddhism in Germany; and a few dozen at our U.S. monasteries in New York and California.) So, in 2008, authorities applied heavy pressure to the abbot of Prajna, who originally had invited and welcomed us in, now to turn against and expel us.

In August 2008 a local police order was issued to the 379 monastics, asserting that they were illegal squatters because the owner of the property did not consent to their presence. Right away the monastics sought to prove to local as well as national authorities that their presence was legitimate, showing them all the receipts for the funds our donors had given for the construction of each building. Nevertheless for fourteen months the monks and nuns of Bat Nha Monastery were continually and increasingly harassed.

For the whole month of September 2008, policemen came to the residences from seven to eleven o'clock every night to question and harass the nuns and monks, the vast majority of whom were under thirty years old. Following the extraordinary living example of kindness given by their teacher, Thich Nhat Hanh, our young nuns and monks would exclaim:

"Oh, poor uncle-policemen, because of us you have to work so hard until midnight to investigate. Sisters, brothers, show them your legal papers first, and then let us sing a song for our uncle-policemen."

"Please prepare some tea for our uncle-policemen!"

"Shall we take a souvenir photo with our uncles?"

After a month of unsuccessful attempts to intimidate our monastics with these nightly visits, this particular practice was abandoned.

The authorities then set up several loudspeakers that blasted insults at the residences twenty-four hours a day. Buses of lay friends who arrived for days of mindfulness practice at the monastery were refused entry by police, and bus owners were threatened. (Our friends found ways to climb the walls to get in to practice with us anyway!) The monastics were then forcibly evicted from one building after another and their belongings literally thrown out of their rooms, often into the rain. These 379 young persons squeezed themselves into smaller and smaller places, but still kept on quietly practicing together to cultivate their mindfulness and their spiritual life.

Their electricity and water supplies were cruelly cut off from June to September 2009. One day during that time, a delegation of venerable monks and nuns from Saigon who came to visit were beaten and pelted with excrement by a mob. On that same day a young woman dressed very provocatively was sent to taunt the monks sitting in meditation. When she came into the meditation hall, she was so struck, so impressed, by their energy, she didn't know what to do. An old woman, presumably a leader of the mob, pushed the young woman and demanded, "Why are you just sitting there silently? Say something!" At that moment the monks began their chanting practice, and the young woman burst into tears. After receiving two calls on her cell phone, she left the room.

The monks and nuns endured it all with compassion, thanks to the support of local people who secretly brought thousands of bottles of mineral water each night between one and two A.M. when the policemen were asleep. The skies also sent water, raining down every night into the monastics' collecting containers.

Finally on September 26–27, 2009, the police sent a violent hired mob of two hundred to provoke the monastics in the ugliest possible ways. They planted condoms and sex books in monks' belongings, yelled at them, and dragged them from their rooms in an effort to load them into thirty taxicabs and four trucks rented specially for the occasion. The monks linked their arms together in circles to resist being thrown into the vehicles. Then the females of the mob actually sank so low as to squeeze the monks' genitals. This finally forced the monks to release their locked arms, whereupon they were immediately stuffed into the taxicabs.

Even as the mob dragged them down several sets of stairs from the fourth floor to ground level, beat them, and stuffed them into the cars, these young people—among them a boxing champion from Dak Lak Province—still refrained from fighting back or harming either the thugs or the policemen (who were supposedly absent and unaware of events, but really participating undercover). The taxi drivers drove about a hundred meters until they were just out of view of the monastery, then released the monks, some of whom sneaked back into Prajna, while others started walking with all the nuns out on the road. The young woman who had been sent in sexy clothing and then cried in the meditation hall now showed up with a huge bag of cookies for them.

That night the monks and nuns walked eighteen kilometers in a heavy rainstorm to Phuoc Hue monastery where they were given refuge. Every fifteen minutes the police telephoned to threaten the abbot of Phuoc Hue in an effort to get him to expel the Prajna monastics from his temple. This abbot bravely resisted for over two months, up to and beyond December 9, 2009, when the mob showed up again to verbally and physically abuse Thay's students—even in the presence of a human rights investigative committee from the European Union, which witnessed the entire incident.

In November 2009 the authorities declared that if our monks and nuns had other monasteries that would take them in, they would be allowed to continue their practice in those other locations. The authorities thought no one would dare try to house and feed such a large number of young people. Then a few months later, when two large monasteries—Toan Duc in Dong Nai Province and Van Hanh in Dalat—decided to welcome us, their proposals were rejected by the authorities.

On December 17, the Prajna monastics heard the police were planning to mobilize some prisoners who would shave their heads and come wearing monks' robes on December 31 to beat our monks and nuns until they left Phuoc Hue. Rather than be part of such a violation of the sacred monastic robe, the monks and nuns finally decided to leave their refuge at Phuoc Hue and quietly emigrate to Cambodia, Thailand, Malaysia, and Hong Kong to seek refuge, even though they lacked any visas. It is the Thi Kinh story once again, as our monks and nuns stayed true to their practice of doing no harm, no violence, even by words, as they withdrew from Vietnam.

Shortly after the forced departure from Vietnam, a temporary home for all the Prajna monastics became available in Thailand, and nine months later Thay came to visit them there. At a gathering of these refugee monastics plus four hundred laypeople from Vietnam, our Thay declared, "This is a genuinely happy moment.

I feel that we are very fortunate. We are going through all these hardships, but our hearts' compassion remains intact; we harbor no anger, not a single wish of retaliation or harm to anyone."

At the very time that Thay was speaking in Thailand, a strong typhoon was flooding several provinces in Vietnam, killing people and destroying crops and houses. Drawing on the typhoon as a metaphor for the monks' and nuns' situation, Thay said, "There are floods in Vietnam. Never mind. We all come over to this safe and dry place. When the floods retreat, we will be back home." All the listeners had tears in their eyes as this old monk's profound compassion penetrated their very being.

Many plays in the form of popular musical theater (*hat cai luong* in South Vietnam, *hat cheo, hat ke chuyen* in North Vietnam) as well as many popular Buddhist storytellers in temples have presented the life of Quan Am Thi Kinh with respect and admiration as a real-life manifestation of the Bodhisattva of Great Compassion, Avalokiteshvara. Everyone hates Mau as the most crude and despicable person. But Thich Nhat Hanh's retelling of the story is in my opinion the expression of his own lived experiences of being unfairly treated and his teaching that compassion extends to everyone, as evidenced by his empathy even for Thien Si and Mau among the characters in the story.

Reading this story increases our capacity for love and understanding toward any and every being, the "bad" as well as the "good." We don't need to feel contempt toward Thien Si; we don't bear anger or hatred toward Thi Mau. We can feel we are one with every person in the story. I have read this story as told by Thay several times, and every time I do, I feel as though I'm reading it for the first time. The last time I read it, it touched me so deeply inside that tears flooded my eyes. I told myself I must read it every week to continually remind myself not to look at things superficially, as has happened in the past.

I could be Thien Si, so shallow, self-centered, and easily carried away by strong personalities like his controlling, jealous mother. How many of us have allowed ourselves to be pulled along, just like Thien Si, by the worst in other people who cannot run their own lives in a proper way? Many of us could be like Mau—proud, reckless, collapsing in our own shame and cowardice, and lying even while another person is severely punished for our own misdeeds. And the council chairman using "moral" authority to judge everyone else—we could be like that too.

Looking back on my life, I see there were many times when I did not know how to look deeply into many conflicts in families and society, to have more understanding and more ability to respond helpfully. The story of Thi Kinh is only the beginning of my training to look more deeply into things that seem obviously "true," but later turn out to be wrong. I train myself to remember Thi Kinh and ask questions. Am I, are we, behaving shallowly like Thien Si, out of weakness or fear of judgment? Am I, are we, letting strong personalities pull us in a wrong direction? Am I, are we, acting like Mau, blinded by arrogance due to too many gifts and successes, losing our way?

Sometimes it can seem as though we've gone too far to turn around. Our society is like that everywhere. I must train myself to make room, to make the time and space, for taking a deeper look into myself and into the person I am interacting with and perhaps judging. There is always room for more understanding, and I train myself to see the deeper truth of each situation. I know that peace in this world is possible if we train ourselves to take a deeper look, especially into people or actions we want to punish because they seem so obviously wrong and deserving of blame. When understanding arises, we can love, we can embrace and be compassionate toward even the worst people, because we see that their weaknesses are also our own. This is how Thay has been able to find so much energy to look directly at the most vicious and virulent acts of violence in our world and work for peace for nearly seventy years, with very little suffering. Let us all embrace wholeheartedly Thay's practice and be his continuation, starting today.

# PRACTICING LOVE

## by Thich Nhat Hanh

Whenever the monks and nuns of Plum Village open a large retreat, a day of mindfulness, or a public talk for many people, we always begin by offering a chant of taking refuge in the great compassion of Quan Am, Avalokiteshvara. This chant invariably moves the hearts of many in attendance, often to tears. When we chant or when we bow down and touch the Earth in homage to Quan Am, in fact we are getting in touch with the energy of boundless love in ourselves. We see we also have the capacity to listen deeply, to love and to understand. First of all, we listen to ourselves, in order to hear ourselves and love ourselves; because if we cannot understand and love ourselves, how will we have the energy to love and understand others?

There are days when you feel nothing seems to work out. You rely on your intelligence, on your talent, and think you can succeed just on that. But there are days when everything seems to go wrong. When things go wrong you try harder, and when you try harder, things continue to go wrong. You say, "This is just not my day." The best thing to do is to stop struggling, go home to yourself, and recover yourself. Don't just keep slogging on, counting on your talent and intelligence to make things right. You have to go home and reestablish your solidity, freedom, peace, and calm before you try again.

In 1964, I helped found the School of Youth for Social Service (SYSS) in Vietnam. It was created during the war to help with the problems of violence, poverty, sickness, and social injustice. We trained young monks, nuns, and laypeople to do social work.

There were some villages with no schools, where the children had to work from a very young age to help their parents cultivate the land, go out fishing, and do many other things; they had no opportunity to get an education. We went to these villages and set up very humble schools. We did not have any money. Just one or two of us would go and play with the children and begin to teach them how to read and write.

When it rained, we would ask one of the villagers for permission to use a house to continue teaching. Gradually the parents could see that the children liked us. Finally, we proposed that people in the village help us to build a school. The school would be made of bamboo and coconut leaves—coconut leaves for the roof and bamboo for the walls. It would be the first school ever built in the village. When people saw that we were doing a good thing, then they helped us make the school bigger, so that other children could come. We also offered classes in the evenings for the children and adults who could not attend class during the day. We found friends who donated oil or kerosene, so we could light lamps for night classes. We began with what we knew and the few resources we had. We did not expect anything from the government, because if you wait for the government, you will wait a long time.

Sometimes we would bring a lawyer or judge from the city to the village, so that the villagers could get birth certificates for their children. If the children did not have birth certificates, they could not enroll in public school. On one morning we might issue twenty birth certificates, and the children who had attended our school could then go to a public school.

We also set up health centers made of coconut-leaf roofs and bamboo walls. We mixed mud with straw and made the walls very warm. I showed the young people how to do it. We also put some cement in it to make it stronger. We asked six students who were about to graduate from medical school to come each week to help diagnose and treat the peasants. Villagers came to the center with all kinds of diseases including cataracts, coughs, and colds. We did not have a budget; we only had our hearts. We were young, and it was the energy of love that helped us do these things.

We also showed people how to build toilets. Up until then, they went to the toilet in many places. If they had diarrhea, the bacteria could get into the water supply, and then other people would get diarrhea. We showed them how to use cement and sand in order to make a very cheap toilet. We also taught people how to make compost and how to raise chickens. We learned the techniques at school and then went into the countryside and shared our knowledge. We did a lot of things like this, and we had a lot of joy.

We also helped form cooperatives and taught people how to organize themselves and invest their money. One person would borrow money from the other families in order to build a house or to invest in a small business. Then the next month another person would be able to borrow money from others.

In this way, we set up pilot project villages. When we arrived at the village, we took photographs of how the people were living. Then, after a year of work and the transformation of the village, we took more photos. We invited peasants from other villages to come and see, so they would be inspired to transform their villages in the same way. We didn't rely on any government, because there were two governments at that time in Vietnam—one Communist and one anti-Communist—and they were fighting each other. We did not want to take sides, because we knew that if we took one side, we would have to fight the other side. When you invest your time and your life in fighting, you cannot help people.

This is a difficult stand to take, because in a situation of conflict, if you align yourself with one warring party, you are protected at least by that party, but if you don't align with either side, you are subject to attack from both parties. When we reminded each side that the other side was not evil and was nothing other than human beings like themselves, we were met with extreme hostility and exposed, my students as well as myself personally, to many dangerous situations. And the pattern has continued from the 1960s all the way up to this day. If I am still sitting here alive today, that is a true miracle, because many of my friends and students were killed.

During the war, bombing destroyed many villages, creating so many desperate refugees. At the beginning, we had planned to work in rural development, but when the war became so intense, we instead took care of refugees and tried to resettle them. In 1969 a village that we had helped build in Quang Tri Province was bombed. It was very close to the Demilitarized Zone (DMZ) separating the North and the South. The village is called Tra Loc. We had spent more than a year making the village into a beautiful place, where people enjoyed living. Then one day American planes came and bombed the village. They had received information that Communist guerrillas had infiltrated it.

The people in the village lost their homes, and our workers took refuge in other places. They sent word to us and asked whether they should rebuild the village, and we said, "Yes, you have to rebuild the village." We spent another six months rebuilding, and then the village was destroyed for a second time by bombing. Again, the people lost their homes. We had built many villages like that throughout the country, but it was very difficult near the DMZ. Then our workers asked us whether we should rebuild it a third time, and after much deliberation we said, "Yes, we have to rebuild it." So we rebuilt it for the third time. Do you know what happened? It was destroyed for a third time by American bombing.

We were very close to despair. Despair is the worst thing that can happen to a human being. We had built the village for the third time, and it was bombarded for the third time. The same question was asked: "Should we rebuild? Or should we give up?" There was a lot of discussion at our headquarters, and the idea of giving up was very tempting—three times was too much. But, in the end, we were wise enough not to give up. If we gave up on Tra Loc village, we would be giving up hope. We had to maintain hope in order not to fall into despair. That is why we decided to rebuild it for the fourth time.

I remember sitting in my office at the Institute of Buddhist Studies in Saigon when a group of young people came to me and asked, "Thay, do you think that the war will end someday? Is there any hope?" Tra Loc village was just one place where the situation was very hard. People were killing each other and dying every day. There were Communists, anti-Communists, Russians, Chinese, and war personnel. Vietnam had become the victim of an international conflict. We wanted to end the war, but we could not, because the situation was not in our hands—it was in the hands of big powers.

"Thay, is there any hope?" Imagine my sitting there, with eighteen young people asking me that question. It seemed as though there was no hope, because the war had been dragging on and on. There was no light at the end of the tunnel. When I was asked that question, I had to practice mindful breathing and going back to my true home—the island of self.

Finally, very calmly, I said, "My dear friends, the Buddha said that everything is impermanent, nothing can last forever. The war also is impermanent; the war will end sometime. Let us not lose hope."

That is what I told them. I did not have a lot of hope myself, I have to confess; but if I'd had no hope, I would have destroyed these young people. I had to practice and nourish a little hope, so that I could be a refuge for them.

The conditions I'm describing here may sound like something very rare and extreme. But in fact there are all kinds of battles being fought all over the world every single day. Some of them do involve bombs and guns. But millions of us who live far from what are normally considered "war zones" are also facing many battles—in our work lives, our communities, and even our own families—and are overwhelmed with anger, resentment, fear, and grief, though we may pretend otherwise. If you yourself are not in such a situation, most likely someone close to you is.

People ask me how I manage not to give in to anger and despair when confronted with great violence and injustice. I think everyone is a victim. If you are not a victim of this, you are a victim of that. For example, when you are full of rage and fear, you are a victim of your rage and fear, and you suffer very deeply. Having a bomb physically explode next to you can make you suffer, that is certainly true; but living day after day with rage and fear makes you suffer also—maybe even more.

We may be abused by others, but we also may be the victims of ourselves. We tend to believe that our enemy is outside of us, but very often we are our own worst enemy because of what we have done to our bodies and our minds. Some people who find themselves in a very difficult situation do not let rage or anxiety take over their minds, and that is why they don't suffer as much as other people in the same situation. Since they are not victims of anger and fear, their minds remain calm and clear, and they can do something to help change the situation.

The people running repressive governments are victims also—victims of their own anger, frustration, and limiting ideas about how to attain safety and security. They are victims of the idea that violence and punishment will make their opponents drop their resistance and violence. That is why helping these people remove the obstacles in their minds not only helps them; it helps everyone. I propose that we look deeply in order to identify our true enemy. For me, our true enemy is our way of thinking—blinded by our pride, anger, and despair.

Whenever there is violence, usually both parties are victims of these kinds of ideas and emotions. The practice recommended in Plum Village is not to destroy the human being, but to destroy the real enemy that is inside the human being. If you want to help someone with tuberculosis, you kill the bacteria, not the person. All of us are victims of the bacteria called violence and wrong perception.

In Plum Village we have helped small groups of Israelis and Palestinians to sit down together, locate the real enemy, and discuss how to remove it. When you still have a lot of anger, fear, and despair, you are not lucid or calm, and you're not able to undertake the right action that can bring real peace. These retreats were deeply moving and very successful, and after the groups went back to the Middle East, they began to actively work to bring greater understanding and reconciliation to the people living around them.

I had a student, Sister Tri Hai, a nun who had graduated from Indiana University in Bloomington with a degree in English literature. After she went back to Vietnam and worked for peace and human rights, she was caught, arrested, and put into prison. Right there in prison, in her small cell, she practiced walking meditation, and she also shared that practice of cultivating inner peace with several other women. In order to keep her courage up so she could survive, she had to practice walking meditation. She had been taught by me how to do mindful walking, to be in the present moment, to nourish herself and her hope. She was able to help many people in prison develop their own source of spiritual strength.

In a situation like that, you survive through your spiritual life; otherwise you will go insane, because you have no hope, you are frustrated, and you suffer so much. That's why the spiritual dimension of your life is so important. Without it you are overwhelmed by anger, despair, and fear, and you cannot help yourself, so how can you help other people? Anger is fire; fear, despair, and suspicion are fire; and they continue to burn you. We have gone through the fire, and we know how hot it is.

Sister Tri Hai practiced walking meditation all night so she could keep herself together and not lose herself in the fire. She went back to her true home within herself. Her true home is not in Paris, London, or Tra Loc, because that home can be bombarded or taken away. Your true home is within yourself. The Buddha said, "Go home to the island within yourself. There is a safe island of self inside. Every time you suffer, every time you are lost, go back to your true home. Nobody can take that true home away from you." This was the ultimate teaching the Buddha gave to his disciples when he was eighty years old and on the verge of passing away.

Many years ago I had a hermitage in a wood, about two hours' drive from Paris. One morning I left the hermitage to go for a walk. I spent the whole day out there, had a picnic lunch, practiced sitting meditation, and wrote poetry. It was very beautiful in the morning, but by late afternoon I noticed that clouds were gathering and the wind was beginning to blow, so I walked back home. When I got there, my hermitage was a mess, because in the morning I had opened all the windows and the door, so that the sunshine could come in and dry everything inside. During my absence the wind had blown all the papers off my desk and scattered them everywhere. The hermitage was cold and desolate.

The first thing I did was to close the windows and the door. The second thing I did was to make a fire. When the fire began to glow, the sound of the wind became joyful for me, and I felt much better. The third thing I did was to pick up all the scattered sheets of paper, put them on the table, and put a stone on them as a paperweight. I spent twenty minutes doing that. Then, finally, I sat down close to the woodstove. The hermitage had become warm and pleasant, and I felt cozy and wonderful inside.

When you find that your conditions are miserable because the windows of your eyes and ears have been left open for too long, the wind from outside is blowing in, and you have become a victim—a mess in your feelings, your body, and your perceptions—you should not keep trying harder and harder to do what you've been trying to do. Go home to your hermitage; it is always there inside you. Close the doors, light the fire, and make it cozy again. That's what is meant by "taking refuge in the island of self." If you don't go home to yourself, you continue to lose yourself in the storms of outside circumstances. You can destroy yourself and the people around you, even if you have good intentions and want to do something to help. That's why the practice of going home to the island of self is so important. No one can take your true home away.

I was exiled from Vietnam from 1966 to 2005. Both the anti-Communists and Communists did not want me to go home. So I learned to find my true home within myself. Wherever I go, I feel at home. Don't think that my home is the hermitage in Plum Village, where I'm living now. My home is more solid than Plum Village, because I know Plum Village can be taken away from us. There have been times when one building or another in Plum Village was shut down by the French government, because we did not meet the building codes—we were too poor or uninformed to have built a fire road, to have certain types of doors, the kitchen built a certain way, and so on. But when that happened, we didn't suffer too much, because we had our true home inside.

If they come and burn your hut and chase you away, of course you suffer; but if you know how to go back to your true home, you will not lose your faith. You know that if your true home is still there inside, you will be able to build another home outside, as when we rebuilt Tra Loc village four times. It is only if you lose your home inside that you lose hope.

Dear friend, please do your best to live your life like Quan Am Thi Kinh. Come back to your true home, the island of your true self. Help your family, your friends, your coworkers to restore their hope, their joy, their peace, and their happiness and reconcile with their family and society. I have great hope that you will be a continuation of the Buddha and bring the light, the practice, joy, and peace to many people. I deeply feel that the Buddha, Jesus, Muhammad, and all our spiritual teachers of many generations are behind you, supporting you, and would like you to continue their work into the future for the sake of all the living beings on this planet.

Thich Nhat Hanh has retreat communities in south-western France (Plum Village), New York (Blue Cliff Monastery), and California (Deer Park Monastery), where monks, nuns, laymen, and laywomen practice the art of mindful living. Visitors are invited to join the practice for at least one week. For information, please write to:

Plum Village
13 Martineau
33580 Dieulivol
France
NH-office@plumvillage.org (for women)
LH-office@plumvillage.org (for women)
UH-office@plumvillage.org (for men)
www.plumvillage.org

For information about our monasteries, mindfulness practice centers, and retreats in the United States, please contact:

Blue Cliff Monastery
3 Hotel Road
Pine Bush, New York 12566
Tel: (845) 733-4959
www.bluecliffmonastery.org

Deer Park Monastery
2499 Melru Lane
Escondido, CA 92026
Tel: (760) 291-1003
Fax: (760) 291-1172
www.deerparkmonastery.org
deerpark@plumvillage.org